OPERATION: CLEAN SWEEP

"Saved by the Bell" titles include:

Mark-Paul Gosselaar: Ultimate Gold
Mario Lopez: High-Voltage Star
Behind the Scenes at "Saved by the Bell"
Beauty and Fitness with "Saved by the Bell"
Dustin Diamond: Teen Star
The "Saved by the Bell" Date Book

Hot new fiction titles:

OPERATION: CLEAN SWEEP

by Beth Cruise

Collier Books
Macmillan Publishing Company
New York
Maxwell Macmillan Canada
Toronto
Maxwell Macmillan International
New York   Oxford   Singapore   Sydney

Collier Books
Macmillan Publishing Company
866 Third Avenue
New York, NY 10022

Maxwell Macmillan Canada, Inc.
1200 Eglinton Avenue East
Suite 200
Don Mills, Ontario M3C 3N1

Macmillan Publishing Company is part of the Maxwell Communication Group of Companies.
First Collier Books edition 1994
Printed in the United States of America
10 9 8 7 6 5 4 3 2 1
Library of Congress Cataloging-in-Publication Data
Cruise, Beth.
Operation clean sweep / by Beth Cruise. — 1st Collier Books ed.
p.   cm.
Summary: On one eventful night Zack, Kelly, and Jessie all go on blind dates, with unexpected and disastrous results.
ISBN 0-02-042793-X
[1. Dating (Social customs)—Fiction.] I. Title.
PZ7.C88827Op 1994
[Fic]—dc20   94-26355

To
all the
"Saved by the Bell"
fans who have ever
gone on a blind date

Chapter 1

▲ ▼ ▲ ▼ ▲

Zack Morris paused on the front steps of Bayside High and peered over the top of his sunglasses at Phyllis Ptowski and her miniskirt as she passed him. The big game against arch rival Valley High was just days away, and he still hadn't decided which lucky lady to take to the big dance afterward.

Reviewing the prospects was an exhausting business, but a man had to do what a man had to do.

Maybe he should take Phyllis. Once she had bid fifty big ones to spend a romantic evening with him. She was gorgeous. Her eyes were big, brown, and worshiping.

Plus, Phyllis was fun to be with. But she wasn't Kelly Kapowski.

It didn't matter that he and Kelly had decided to just be friends. He'd been in love with her for so long, it was hard to break the habit. Besides, he wasn't sure he even wanted to break the habit. It had been great to have the nicest, most beautiful girl at school as his steady.

But no more, Zack reminded himself. Now Zack Morris was a free man, and the world was full of girls who were knockouts. All he had to do was put his mind to the task at hand, and the problem of who to take to the dance would be solved. After all, there wasn't a girl alive who could resist his dazzling smile and blond good looks.

"Hi, Zack," Betsy Bellamy, a pretty blond, greeted him. "Looking for someone?" She hugged her textbooks to her chest and gave him a slow, flirtatious smile.

"Yeah," Zack said. "You see Jessie Spano anywhere?" Jessie had lived next door to him nearly forever and was one of his best friends.

The voltage of Betsy's smile lessened at the mention of another girl's name. The look in her baby blue eyes turned arctic. "Nope, sorry." She turned sharply on her heel and strode off toward the student parking lot.

Major error, Morris, Zack told himself. If he kept this up, not only wouldn't he have a date for Friday night, there wouldn't be a girl alive at Bayside who would give him the time of day.

A hand landed on his shoulder, making Zack stagger.

"What's the matter, preppie? Losing your touch?" A. C. Slater demanded with a grin. His deep dimples flashed, causing Cathie Lynn Carmody, the nerdiest girl at Bayside, to feel so faint that she forgot the rest of the algebraic equation she was explaining to Alan Zobel and nearly walked into a tree.

"Dream on, Slater," Zack said. "There's just so many deserving girls and so little of me to go around. What about you? Who are you taking to the dance?"

Slater shrugged his muscular shoulders. He was captain of both the football and wrestling teams and worked out regularly. "I'm playing this like I would a football game," he said. "I'm keeping the field open so I can intercept any and all passes."

"Going stag, huh?" Zack pressed.

"No way."

Daisy Tyler, one of the Bayside cheerleaders, dashed past them. "Hi, guys," she called, giving both Zack and Slater her brightest smile before disappearing inside the school.

"Maybe you should have asked her out," Slater suggested.

"I didn't want to hurt your chances, pal," Zack insisted. "Why didn't *you* ask her?"

"Maybe I will later," Slater said. "Right now I'm in major need of a mondo cheeseburger with the works."

Zack's stomach growled at the mention of food. "Last one to the Max buys the fries," he called, already at a run.

Slater ended up buying. The muscle-bound cretin might be boss on the football field, Zack thought with pleasure, but he couldn't match the speed of a man with a letter in track. Especially when that man was Zack Morris, master scammer and blazer of a zillion shortcuts.

Still, Zack was gasping for breath when he reached the Max. The rest of his friends were already there and sipping on colas. Fortunately for him, the seat next to Kelly Kapowski was empty. Zack slid smoothly into the spot as if it had been saved specially for him.

Slater came through the door barely five seconds later, but it was enough of a margin to make a big difference in Zack's wallet. "I'll have the super jumbo fries with nacho cheese," he told the waitress, "and put them on my friend Slater's bill."

"Hi, Zack," Kelly said, and handed him a bunch of napkins to wipe the sweat from his face. "You'll need a humongous cola with all those fries."

"So true," he agreed. She was so sweet! Always thinking about her fellow man. If only he could be the *only* fellow man she thought about!

"You, too, Slater," Kelly said as he squeezed into the booth next to Jessie. She passed another bunch of napkins across the table to him. "We can't have our star football player getting weak with the big game coming up this week."

"That's right! Maybe you'd better have a triple burger to keep up your strength," Lisa Turtle suggested. "I've been agonizing over what to wear to the dance so much that I'm losing sleep. If I thought you were too weak to play, I'd *never* get to sleep, and I'd end up with really gross circles under my eyes. Then I wouldn't be able to set foot out of my room, much less the house!"

Fashion and looking good were sciences to Lisa, ones she studied diligently.

"Don't worry, Lisa," Samuel "Screech" Powers declared in his squeaky voice. He had been nuts about Lisa for years. "I'll still love you, even if you wear zinc oxide to hide those circles."

"Ewwww," Lisa said, wrinkling her nose in disgust.

"I don't think it will come to that, Screech," Jessie Spano assured him. "Besides, from the things I've heard lately about the Valley High team, we might not have a victory to celebrate, whether Slater plays or not."

"Whoa! Back up, momma," Slater insisted. "What do you mean? We're going to tromp them. Trust me."

"I trust you, Slater," Screech chirped brightly, then turned to Jessie, his flexible face becoming serious. "But just in case, do you think I should wear my elephant safari T-shirt? Valley isn't known as the Mastodons for nothing, you know. I'd like them to think kindly of me."

The gang ignored him and leaned forward over the table, anxious to hear what Jessie had learned.

"What did you hear?" Kelly asked. She was the head cheerleader for Bayside and was behind the team one hundred percent.

"I'm sorry, Slater," Jessie said. "But I heard this from a very reputable source. Shelly Danforth, who is one of the girls in my Green Teens group, says that her cousin Cindy's best friend's fiancé's younger brother is in the Valley quarterback's math class and he claims they have some awesome new plays guaranteed to crush Bayside this year."

"Oh noooo!" Lisa wailed. "I just knew disaster was in the air when I broke a nail in English this morning."

"It can't be that bad," Zack said. "Can it?" He looked at Slater, hoping to see his friend oozing with confidence despite the bad news.

But Slater was looking a little green. And he hadn't even bitten into his triple patty Max-imum burger yet.

"What kind of plays?" Slater asked. His voice was a bit strangled.

"I don't know," Jessie confessed. "Shelly knows about as much about football as I do. She did say something about a switch on the old Statue of Liberty play. Does that make sense to you?"

From the expression on Slater's face, Zack figured it made perfect sense to his buddy.

"Oh, Slater," Kelly cried softly. Her tender heart went out to all the wrong people as far as Zack was concerned. "If only the Valley team could have lost as many of its experienced players as their cheerleading squad did."

"Yeah," Slater groaned. After a moment, Kelly's news sank in. "What do you mean?"

"Didn't you know? So many of Valley's best cheerleaders graduated last year, nearly their whole squad is made up of new girls. Ms. Pachinko said we have a good chance of winning the citywide cheerleading competition this year because Valley is building almost from scratch. Only one girl from last year's group remained, so they made her the head cheerleader since she was the only one with any experience."

"Wow," Screech said. "That's terrible for them."

"But good for us," Slater pointed out. "At least for our cheerleaders. I just wish we knew what their new plays were. But there is no way we could ever find out now. The locker room at Valley will be tighter than Fort Knox."

"They have a special knock?" Screech squeaked.

"Pul-eeese," Lisa groaned. "Next you'll be telling knock-knock jokes."

"I know some great ones, babe," Screech told

her, moving his eyebrows up and down.

"Help!" Lisa whispered to Kelly.

Zack finished off his fries and thoughtfully rubbed ketchup off his chin with his napkin. "We need a plan," he said.

"Maybe we could get Denny Vane to cripple Valley's quarterback," Slater suggested.

Jessie frowned at him. "Get real, Slater. Denny may dress like a hood, but you know he's one of the sweetest people in the world."

"Why the quarterback?" Zack asked.

"Have you been paying attention, preppie?" Slater growled. "He's the guy calling the new plays."

"But he's got the same old team running them," Zack reminded him. "All we have to do is demoralize them."

"Yeah, right." Slater looked a bit demoralized himself.

Jessie's hazel eyes narrowed in suspicion, though. "What are you thinking, Zack?"

"Me?"

"Don't try that innocent act with us, Zack Morris," Lisa said. "We know you too well, sweetie."

Zack felt excitement run through his veins just at the idea of pulling a new scam. And this one would benefit not just him but everyone at good old Bayside High.

"What gets you motivated during a game?" he asked Slater casually.

"That's easy. Coach Sonski's pep talks."

"And what else?" Zack pushed calmly.

"The yells of the fans."

"And?" Zack's voice was a little more impatient now.

Slater leaned back in the booth. "Seeing the cheerleaders jumping around in those short skirts and kicking up their great legs." He sighed dreamily.

"Bingo!" Zack agreed.

"Bingo? I love to play!" Screech said. "I go with my grandmother each Wednesday and . . ."

Jessie frowned. "Cheerleaders? Is that all you Neanderthals think about?"

Slater considered the question a moment. "Yes," he said.

Jessie took a deep breath, ready to argue about the sexist views held by football players.

"So, do you have a plan, Zack?" Kelly asked before Jessie could get started.

"Doesn't he always?" Lisa said.

"Lay it on me, preppie," Slater urged. "I need some good news."

Zack stretched in his seat, his arm casually dropping along the back of the bench behind Kelly. "Oh, it's nothing much," he said. "I just propose that we pull the rug out from under Valley's team."

"They'll be standing on a rug? Won't it get dirty on the field?" Screech demanded.

"I say we remove the one person who can keep

morale up for the Mastodons," Zack explained. "All we have to do is kidnap Valley's head cheerleader. The rest, as they say, will be history."

Chapter 2

▲ ▼ ▲ ▼ ▲

"*Kidnap a cheerleader?*" Jessie gasped. "That's a criminal offense."

"Okay, don't call it kidnapping. Think of it more as delaying her arrival," Zack urged. "We'll buy her dinner. Can we help it if the food arrives at the same time the game starts? Can we help it if the service is so bad that the game is over by the time we finish dessert?"

"Heck, no," Screech said. "But there's no way that waiter is going to get a big tip. I might not even go to that restaurant ever again."

Slater frowned. "I don't know, Zack. Who's this *we*? I'm playing football, so I can't be kidnapping some cheerleader."

"You can't kidnap a girl . . ." Jessie began.

"We'll be sidetracking her," Zack corrected hastily.

"I can't help, either," Kelly said. "I have to lead the cheers for the Bayside team."

Slater's deep dimples flashed in a grin. "Yeah, you know, Zack. Building our morale by jumping up and down in those short skirts."

Jessie gritted her teeth, holding back a stinging remark. A strangled sound escaped her throat.

"You okay, momma?" Slater asked. Amusement danced in his brown eyes. He'd been fielding Jessie's zingers for a long time. He knew she couldn't keep from laying into him for much longer.

"I'm fine," Jessie croaked. "But I can't help, either. I know this game is important, but so is the special meeting of Green Teens Friday night. I was just going to go to the dance afterward. Sorry, gang, but I can't miss this meeting. It's really important."

Green Teens was Jessie's environmentally concerned group. The good of the world always came first with Jessie. Even when it came to the Bayside vs. Valley game.

Lisa's eyes grew wide and defensive as everyone turned to her. "Don't look at me," she insisted. "I'm a cheerleader, too. I can't let the team down by not being at the game."

Zack sighed theatrically. "Then I guess it's up to me."

"Fear not, kemosabe," Screech announced. "I won't let you down. I'll be your right-hand man. Your partner, your pal, your backup. I'll be there when you need me. Should we synchronize our watches?"

The gang exchanged glances.

"If I were you, preppie," Slater whispered to Zack across the table, "I think I'd come up with a Plan B. And I'd do it fast."

▲ ▼ ▲

Jessie's blue Toyota had barely come to a stop in the mall parking lot when Lisa was out of her seat. Kelly and Jessie were a heartbeat behind her. They knew better than to lag behind when Lisa hit the mall. Shopping was serious business with their friend.

"Do you know who you're going to the dance with, Lisa?" Kelly asked.

"No, not yet," Lisa answered. "It would be terrible to miss the victory celebration, but no way am I going alone. What about you, Kelly?"

Jessie laughed softly as they entered the center court of the mall. It was like being in the middle of a bicycle wheel with stores spread out on spokes all around them. "Perhaps the question should be who hasn't asked her! Now that you're not going steady with anybody, I don't think there is a single boy at Bayside who hasn't asked you out, Kelly."

Kelly moaned. "Oh, I know. It's terrible!"

"The rest of us should be so unfortunate," Jessie said.

Lisa paused, considering each wing of the mall

carefully. Which of her favorite stores should she hit first? There was a sale on at Beaucoup Bargains, but she'd seen the cutest outfit in the window at Très Charmant a couple of days ago. She'd been dreaming of it ever since.

"Didn't Butch Henderson pin *you* against your locker the other day?" Lisa asked Jessie. Butch was a stocky fullback on the Bayside team.

"He tried," Jessie said with a grin. "But can you really see me with that caveman? He's worse than Slater. At least Slater has some brains. Few, but some."

"What about Ron Noland? I saw you talking to him in the cafeteria," Kelly said. Ron was president of the chess club, wore glasses, and seemed far more likely to be Jessie's intellectual equal.

Jessie sighed. "He wanted my opinion on the tofu burgers Ms. Meadows was serving."

"Ron's nice, but he certainly can't be considered in the running," Lisa announced. "He's a full head shorter than you, girl, and a fashion wasteland on top of that."

Kelly giggled. "Moe of the Three Stooges is his idol. But seriously, are you going to the dance with anyone, Jessie?"

"Yes I am. But you don't know him. Actually, *I* don't even know him," Jessie admitted.

Lisa's eyes widened in surprise as she momentarily forgot about shopping. But then, boys were her other hobby. "You mean, you've got a blind date? How exciting!"

"How romantic!" Kelly agreed enthusiastically. "Who is he?"

Jessie's eyes glowed with pleasure. "A new member of Green Teens."

"So that's why this meeting is so special. Here I thought you were going to be organizing another march to save the whales," Lisa said.

Kelly pulled Jessie down on a nearby bench. "So tell us everything you know about him! What's his name?"

"Well," Jessie began. "His parents are superhippies from the sixties. They named him Sequoia Forrest, but I don't know a whole lot about him other than that. He and his sister were mega-involved with the Green Teens chapter in northern California, but they're new to Palisades. Shelly Danforth told me about him. She's going to officially introduce us at the emergency meeting Friday night."

Lisa nodded sagely. "Meeting a new hunk certainly qualifies the meeting as an emergency."

Kelly sighed. "I'll bet he's tall and strong like a sequoia tree. You two will have so much in common, too. I'm so happy for you, Jessie."

"Maybe you should wait to congratulate me," Jessie said with a laugh. "He just might be too good to be true."

"I know Sequoia will be the perfect guy for you,"

Kelly said wistfully. "It's like Shelly is your fairy god-mother. With a wave of her magic wand, she has presented you with a prince who will sweep you off your feet, he'll be so charming."

"Charming," Lisa echoed. "Oh my gosh! I almost forgot why we're here! I've got to go try on that cute outfit at Très Charmant. What about you guys?"

Jessie opened her purse and pulled out a list. "Mom has been really busy lately, so I volunteered to run errands for her. What about you, Kelly?"

The pretty brunette tossed her long, shiny hair back over her shoulder and grinned. "I'm just glad I don't have to go to work at Yogurt 4-U today. But I'm trying to save some money, so I can't shop for myself. I'll just tag along with one of you."

"Come tell me what you think about this gorgeous ensemble then," Lisa urged. "We can meet Jessie at the food court for a diet cola."

"In an hour?" Jessie asked.

Lisa gave her a disbelieving look. "More like two," she said. "And that's only if I rush."

▲　▼　▲

Zack had his head in the refrigerator looking for a snack when his mother got home from work.

"Hard day, honey?" Mrs. Morris asked sympathetically.

"No more than usual, Mom," he assured her as he palmed a liter bottle of soda from the fridge and grabbed a bag of chips from the counter. "Why do you ask?"

"Oh, just little things," his mother said. "Your car isn't parked in the center of the driveway, the television isn't blaring ROCK-TV videos, the stereo is still tuned to your father's favorite oldies station, and the kitchen doesn't look like a typhoon swept through it."

"I left wet towels all over the bathroom and dropped dirty clothes on the floor rather than put them in the laundry basket," Zack offered.

Mrs. Morris grinned. "Then it isn't the end of the world after all." She helped herself to a chip and sat down at the kitchen table. "What's the problem? Maybe I can help."

Zack collapsed in the chair across from hers and stretched his legs out. "I don't think so, Mom. I've got to figure out who to take to the dance Friday night."

"Major bummer," Mrs. Morris agreed.

Zack smiled. His mother was sweet, but when she tried to talk like one of the gang, it sounded really weird.

"Really major bummer," he said. "There's so many things to take into consideration."

"I know what you mean, darling. There's whether the girl's interests are similar to yours, if you share the same goals in life, whether—"

"Whether she's a gorgeous babe."

Mrs. Morris nodded. "Absolutely," she agreed, although her blue eyes twinkled with amusement. "Maybe we should order out for pizza so you have sufficient energy to make a decision."

"Pepperoni, pineapple, and anchovies?" Zack asked.

His mother made a face. "Perhaps we'll get a separate pizza for you," she said.

"Even that won't help, though," Zack admitted. "There are a lot of girls at Bayside, but none of them measures up to Kelly. It's impossible to decide who to ask."

"Hmm," Mrs. Morris murmured. She tapped a finger thoughtfully against her cheek. "Maybe I can help you, sweetheart."

Zack wasn't sure he liked the sound of that, but he was desperate enough to take even a parent's advice.

"One of the women where I work—you know Sheila—is seeing a man who has a teenage daughter," Mrs. Morris said.

Zack knew exactly what the daughter would look like. And it wasn't babe city.

"Sheila says Brandon's daughter is darling and very nice."

Zack winced. Nice? The word was like vinegar on his tongue. Kelly Kapowski was nice, but she was also drop-dead gorgeous, an exception to the rule. His mother didn't seem to know it, but she was talking major dog here.

"She's a senior, too, and quite popular at school," Mrs. Morris continued.

Popular? The same could be said about Brenda Tolliver, but her popularity was limited to the nerds in science class.

Zack Morris would never be desperate enough to take out someone like Brenda. Not unless there was something in it for him, that is.

"I believe Sheila said Brandon's daughter is driving a Ferrari at the moment," Mrs. Morris said.

Zack perked up. *A Ferrari?* "What color?" As if it mattered.

"Red, I believe."

Breathing a little easier, Zack relaxed back in his chair. He'd once driven rock star Andy Prime's red Ferrari a total distance of one block before someone crashed into it. That short time behind the wheel had been the closest he'd ever gotten to driving heaven.

"If you'd like, I could call Sheila and see if Brandon's daughter, and her car, are free Friday night," Mrs. Morris offered.

"Could you, Mom? It would take a load off my mind," Zack said humbly. "You're a real pal."

Chapter 3

▲ ▼ ▲ ▼ ▲

Lisa spun in a circle, arms spread to show off the apricot silk miniskirt and matching blouse to advantage. "What do you think?"

"I think your parents will kill you if you spend that much money on one outfit," Kelly said. "But it is beautiful."

Lisa pirouetted before a full-length mirror. "I think you're right. They will kill me. But it's so classic. It's not like it'll be out of style next week." Luckily Lisa's parents were both doctors, so they could afford her expensive taste.

"Now all I have to do is find shoes, a purse, and the right earrings to go with it," Lisa declared. "What are you going to wear to the dance?"

"Me?" Kelly looked unhappy. "I don't think I'll be going. I've had lots of offers from guys at school, yet I just can't work up enough enthusiasm to go out with any of them. Maybe I need to meet someone totally new. Like Jessie's doing."

Lisa popped back into the changing room. "Yeah," she agreed. "We've known all the guys from school for so long that there's no mystery left."

"Lisa?" a woman asked. She had a gorgeous sea green cocktail dress draped over her arm ready to try on. Large diamond rings sparkled on her fingers. "Lisa Turtle?"

"Dr. Vogel?" Lisa's tone echoed the surprise in the woman's voice before she smiled brightly over the changing-room door. "Hi!"

"I thought it was you," the woman said. "But I should have expected to see you in this shop. You have such wonderful taste in clothes."

Lisa hastily finished pulling her own clothes back on and stepped out of the changing room. "That's nice of you to say, Dr. Vogel," she said, and introduced Kelly. "Dr. Vogel is a family counselor. Her office is just down the hall from Mom and Dad's."

"We're all so busy, we rarely get to visit and keep up with each other's families," Dr. Vogel said. "I've been so swamped that I put off finding something to wear to the annual Palisades Family Counselors dinner-dance this weekend. Now I'm feeling desperate. Do you think I could impose on your fashion sense, Lisa?"

Kelly giggled. "It would be hard to stop her, Dr. Vogel."

Lisa glanced at the dress Dr. Vogel had chosen and immediately vetoed it. "Too much green," she decided. "I think I saw just the thing, though. Wait a sec while I find it."

Left alone with Dr. Vogel, Kelly searched for something to say. "It must be wonderful to help troubled families," she said.

Dr. Vogel nodded happily. "I enjoy it. I feel so needed and fulfilled aiding children and their parents with their problems. I also feel very fortunate that my son has shown not only an interest but an aptitude for the same field."

"Oh?" Kelly murmured. She couldn't think of anything else to say. Her own family was large. She had six brothers and sisters. But everyone got along with one another. The Kapowski family was a cheerful and loving one. It was hard for Kelly to imagine what it would be like to have a family that wasn't happy.

"Yes," Dr. Vogel said. "My son Austin is in his second year at California University and majoring in family therapy. I'm so proud of him. He's quite intelligent and very handsome. Would you like to see a picture of him?"

Trapped, Kelly looked around the sales floor frantically, searching for Lisa.

"Here it is," Dr. Vogel declared, and shoved

her open wallet under Kelly's nose.

The displayed picture of Austin Vogel was enough to take Kelly's breath away. His mother hadn't been kidding! He really was handsome!

"I'll bet you and he would get along very well," Dr. Vogel said. "I've tried to match him up with Lisa, but she isn't keen on the idea since my office is so near her parents'. I think she believes we would compare notes or something."

The Turtles were wonderful parents and respected Lisa's privacy, but Kelly was pretty sure Dr. Vogel would be eager to find out every detail she could about her son's dates.

"Austin is coming home for a visit this weekend. With all the preparations for the dinner-dance, I just won't have much time to spend with him. Perhaps you could help, Kelly," Dr. Vogel suggested.

"Me?"

"It would be so nice if you'd let Austin call you. Perhaps you could go to a show together. He'll be home Friday afternoon after his last class."

Dr. Vogel wanted her to go on a blind date? Kelly wasn't quite sure how she felt about the idea. It had sounded romantic when she learned Jessie was going out on one. But was it a good idea for her?

Of course, it wasn't a totally blind date. She at least knew that Austin Vogel was gorgeous.

Besides, what did she have to lose?

"Okay, sure," Kelly said as Lisa emerged from the

clothing racks with a stunning silver-and-white gown in hand. "I'd love to go out with your son, Dr. Vogel."

▲　▼　▲

Zack was halfway out the door Friday night when his mother called him.

"Remember, sweetheart, your date will come by the house, with her Ferrari, around nine-thirty. Will you be back from the football game in time?" she asked.

"Plenty of time," Zack said. Bayside would have pounded Valley into the ground long before then. Especially since they had their own secret play: the Zack Attack.

"You might like to know that her name is—"

"Later, Mom! Gotta go," Zack yelled back, and swung into his '65 Mustang convertible. The radio blasted to life, drowning out everything else. It didn't really matter what his date's name was just as long as she handed him the keys to that boss red Ferrari.

Within minutes, he'd swung by Screech's house and picked up his friend. They synchronized watches and cruised slowly down Surfside Lane toward their victim's home.

Screech sank low in his seat. "What if Brandi Jarrett has already left for the game?" he asked nervously. "What if she's got a bodyguard? What if—"

"Relax, Screech," Zack soothed, scrunching low behind the wheel himself. It wouldn't do to give the scam away too early. They had to take Brandi by surprise. More important, he had to turn on that old Zack charm so she wouldn't suspect a thing until it was too late.

"She hasn't left," he told Screech. "I can see her through the front window."

"You can?" Screech's curly head popped up.

"She's kind of hard to miss with that platinum blond hair and her cheerleading uniform." It was really long hair, too, falling nearly to her waist, its color like that of a moonbeam gleaming off the ocean. That wasn't the most distractingly beautiful thing about Brandi Jarrett, though. The fit of her cheerleading uniform was enough to make any red-blooded boy dizzy.

"Do you think she knows we spied on her? Does she know we followed her home from school?" Screech demanded in a loud whisper.

"Not a chance," Zack assured him. "A secret agent would have envied our cool."

"Right you are, triple-oh-seven."

"Shhh!" Zack hissed as the door to Brandi's house swung open. "Here she comes."

He eased his car door open and scrambled out, balanced and ready for the next move.

Screech got into position on the opposite side of the car, his wild orange-and-green patterned shirt, purple suspenders, and plaid pants almost blending with one of the neighbor's flower gardens.

When Brandi's back was to him, Zack raced to

her side and calmly plucked her car keys from her hand.

"Not tonight, my lady," he said, and flashed one of his most dazzling smiles. Brandi's keys sailed over his shoulder toward the front door of her house.

"We can't have you tiring yourself out by fighting traffic! Allow me," Zack insisted, taking Brandi's elbow in hand and steering her toward his car. Screech snapped to attention, a chauffeur's hat on his head, his face disguised with a pair of shocking-pink-framed sunglasses and a drooping false mustache. He pulled the passenger-side door open and saluted.

Brandi giggled and tossed her shiny hair over her shoulder. "Don't be ridiculous. Who are you anyway? I don't recognize you from school."

Fortunately, Zack thought, that didn't seem to bother her. "I'm an admirer from afar," he said.

He wasn't lying. Bayside was at least five miles from Valley High.

Brandi paused beside the Mustang and gave Zack a flirtatious look beneath her long lashes. "Is that true?"

"Yes," Zack said, then looked sad. "And no," he added sorrowfully. "Actually, the team sent me."

In a way they had, Zack mused. It was just that the Bayside team had sent him, not Valley's.

"How sweet," Brandi declared, and settled into the passenger seat. Zack slid over the hood and behind the wheel in nothing flat. Screech fell into the backseat and nearly lost his mustache when the car shot down the street.

"You missed the turn," Brandi said when Zack headed for the Max. "The football field is the other way."

"But dinner is this way," Zack explained smoothly. "We need you to keep your strength up."

"And you should eat as slowly as you can," Screech piped up, pushing his disguise back in place. "It isn't good for your digestion to gulp down your food. Chew every bite at least twelve times."

"I'll remember that," Brandi told him. "But I'm afraid I'll look like a cow chewing that many times."

"Never, my princess," Zack said. "And if you do, I'll still put the *mooove* on you."

"But I thought we wanted to make her go slow, Zack, not mooove," Screech said, confused.

Mentally, Zack groaned.

Brandi twisted in her seat. "So you're Zack, huh?" she murmured. "Zack what?"

"Ahhh . . ."

"Bond," Screech cried. "Zack Bond. And I'm . . . I'm . . ."

"He's Arnold Benedict," Zack supplied hastily. "When he's excited, he sometimes stutters."

"I do?" Screech sounded amazed.

"We're both new in town," Zack continued, "but we heard that the Max has the best burgers around. Do you know anything about the place?"

Brandi shrugged. "Only that it's a Bayside hangout. But that doesn't matter. They're probably all at the game already."

"They are if they want good seats," Zack said. "But we don't have to worry about that. We've got the best in the house."

"Fifty-yard line," Brandi agreed. "That's where the cheerleaders are. If you're there, too, you must have gotten jobs with the team."

"That's right. I'm their manager."

"And him?" Brandi nodded at Screech, who sat leaning forward, his face right between them.

"Arnold's the towel boy."

Screech grinned widely. "You should see me snap those babies," he said.

"I'll pass on that," Brandi said. "But not on dinner. Suddenly I'm starved. When do we eat?"

Chapter 4

▲ ▼ ▲ ▼ ▲

Jessie squared her shoulders and took a deep breath. It was ridiculous to feel nervous about a Green Teens meeting. She'd always gotten excited when she'd stepped through the doors of the community center meeting room and heard the voices of the other kids discussing important issues. Slater, Kelly, Zack, and the rest of the gang were great friends. They agreed with her that there were things that had to be done to save the earth, but they didn't feel as passionate about it as she did.

That was what was so great about Green Teens. At the monthly meetings, Jessie rubbed shoulders with other teenagers who had the same sense of commitment that she did.

But tonight all she could think about was meeting her blind date.

Jessie rubbed her sweating palms down her jeans to dry them and pulled open the door to the meeting room.

Shelly Danforth pounced on her immediately.

"Jessie! Where have you been? I thought you weren't coming, you're so late!"

Shelly was a tall girl who wore her blond hair cut in a boyish style. There wasn't much else that was boyish about her though, since her laugh was an infectious giggle and her eyes were as big and blue as those of a baby doll. She lived on the opposite side of Palisades and attended a private school, so Jessie didn't see her often. They did talk on the phone a lot, discussing various Green Teen projects. Shelly was the president of the group.

"Well," Jessie admitted, greeting her friend, "I almost got cold feet. I'm not so sure about going on a blind date."

Shelly grinned widely. "Not to worry. Sequoia is absolutely the most gorgeous hunk I've ever seen. If I wasn't going steady myself, I'd jump on the guy."

"I don't know, Shelly," Jessie said, still nervous.

"Just meet him," Shelly urged. "If you still aren't interested, I won't push you. Deal?"

Jessie smiled. "Deal."

"Then come on," Shelly said, and dragged Jessie toward the front of the room.

There were a lot of other teens already gathered near the front table, both boys and girls. Usually everyone milled around in smaller groups. Tonight, though, they looked like a small mob. Maybe someone had brought flyers or information about a new issue, or had created a display that had caught everyone's attention.

Shelly plowed into the crowd, pulling Jessie after her, until they reached the table. There was indeed a display and flyers concerning the removal of desert plants, but it was the tall, broad-shouldered young man bent over the display who caught Jessie's attention.

Although she guessed that he was her age, Jessie didn't think anyone could call this guy a boy. He was nothing like Slater or Zack, who were both tall and good-looking. This hunk was truly a hunk. When he straightened to his full height, he towered over the rest of the Green Teens. He had worn, faded jeans on and a sleeveless T-shirt, both of which hugged muscles that made Slater look like a wimp. His hair was long, curling to his shoulders, and was the color of redwood bark. His eyes were the same shade as moss in a forest.

"Sequoia," Shelly said, "I'd like you to meet Jessie Spano."

The hunk smiled, and Jessie's reservations about him melted. His hand closed around hers. "I've been looking forward to this night, Jessie," he said in a deep voice. "Shelly has told me many good things about your involvement in our crusade to save the planet."

It was great to have a guy appreciate her for her dedication and intelligence, but couldn't Shelly have hinted to *him* that she was gorgeous, too?

"And you are more beautiful than she said you were," Sequoia said.

Jessie's legs went all rubbery at his words. "Thank you. I've been looking forward to meeting you, too, Sequoia."

He smiled down into her eyes. "We have much in common, Jessie Spano. Much to discuss."

Jessie sighed happily. "Yes, we do," she said.

"Then let's get this meeting on the road," Shelly announced. "There's a really good reason why we called this emergency meeting. Everybody take a seat."

Jessie found a chair in the front row and tried to get her mind back on business. Which was difficult since Sequoia took a seat at the front table near Shelly. A moment later, a thin girl with straight long green hair took the chair next to him. She had on a loose-fitting white dress decorated with flowing green ribbons. She wore ballet slippers in a shade of green that matched her hair. Were they going to have some kind of performance? Jessie wondered. Surely the girl didn't usually dress so strangely.

"This special session of Green Teens will please come to order," Shelly said. "I'd like to thank you for coming tonight. It's nice to see so many of you are dedicated to our cause, especially those members who go to Bayside and Valley high schools since they gave up attending the big game to be here."

There were chuckles from the audience, and Jessie found herself grinning widely. But her happiness had nothing to do with Shelly's joke. It was because Sequoia had turned his bright white smile her way.

"I bring you bad news this night, fellow Green Teens," Shelly announced. "A company calling itself Desert Beauty has recently bought a large section of the California desert a half-hour's drive east of Palisades. They may call themselves Desert Beauty, but their goal is to make money by destroying the balance of nature in the desert."

There were murmurs of disapproval around Jessie. She nodded in total agreement with those near her and found Sequoia's approving gaze on her. Her heart started beating a little faster. What girl's heart wouldn't? He was so unbelievably gorgeous!

"But let me introduce you to our newest members, who can tell you more about Desert Beauty's destruction. This is Sequoia Forrest and his sister Evergreen, who recently moved to Palisades from northern California where they had been involved in many Green Teen projects."

Jessie glanced at the green-haired girl once more. She was Evergreen Forrest? Boy! And the gang thought Screech was weird? Next to Evergreen, Screech was almost normal!

Sequoia got to his feet and looked around the room. He began to talk, his voice calm and controlled, although as he described the way the people at Desert Beauty were selling off the desert plants to various landscaping companies, his dark eyes seemed to flash with restrained anger.

"If this practice continues," he declared, "there will be massive erosion. Just as the trees in our forests need to be replaced through reforestation, so too do our deserts need to be preserved. It is possible to have a tall, mature tree within ten or twenty years, but there are some species of cactus that only begin to mature after seventy-five years. By selling off the desert plants, not just the mature cactuses, but also the younger ones, Desert Beauty is quickly destroying what beauty our desert has! Something must be done!"

When he sat down, there was thunderous applause. Jessie was just as fired up as the rest of the audience. She jumped to her feet. "We've got to do something to stop them!" she cried. "And we must do it quickly!"

Sequoia gave her a thumbs-up sign. It made her heart skip a beat.

"All right, who would like to be on the committee to investigate Desert Beauty?" Shelly asked.

Jessie's hand shot up before she realized Sequoia was frowning at her and shaking his head. He didn't want her to work on his project? Why not? She dropped her hand just as quickly, a little embarrassed and disappointed by his action.

"Jessie?" Shelly asked. "Did you want to be one of the committee members?"

Jessie stole a quick glance at Sequoia. Once again he gave a negative shake of his head. "Ah, I just remembered I've got a giant project due at school and don't have much time to spare," she said. It felt terrible to be lying, but until she talked to Sequoia she had no way of knowing why he had discouraged her from volunteering. She could always be involved in whatever protest the committee decided upon. That thought eased her conscience a little.

Shelly finished gathering volunteers and moved on to other Green Teens business. Jessie listened to it all with one ear, her mind busy with the mystery Sequoia presented. But until the meeting was over, all she could do was make guesses about his reasons. It was enough to drive a girl nuts!

▲ ▼ ▲

Brandi snuggled close to Zack's side in the gang's regular booth at the Max. Screech was across from them, finishing off an extra-large order of fries. He'd already inhaled two double-decker burgers, a plate of onion rings, and three strawberry shakes. Zack wondered where his skinny friend put all the food. At the rate he ate, Screech should be as big as Bayside's Clive Quackenbush, who was nearly as wide as he was tall.

Brandi had nibbled at a salad while Zack had contented himself with a regular burger and fries. He had more on his mind than food. A glance at the clock on the wall told him the Bayside vs. Valley game was probably approaching halftime and since Brandi had finished her dinner, he needed a new plan to keep her away from the football field. She'd already turned down dessert, although Screech had looked interested at the mention of a triple-scoop hot fudge sundae with the works.

Screech could easily eat the entire time it took to play the game, but it was Brandi they had to keep busy. What new ploy could he use to delay her? She was such a babe, Zack knew he wouldn't be stumped for ideas if he and Brandi were alone. He could always say he was taking her to the game and then choose a long route that took them past Palisades's many romantic beaches.

Now there was an idea that had merit! All he had to do was get rid of Screech. But first he had to know how the game was going. If Bayside was way out in front point-wise, he could keep Brandi occupied for another hour and then head for the stands to watch the grand finale as Bayside tromped Valley into the dust. Right now, though, he had to find out what the score was.

Brandi sipped the last of her diet cola and gave Zack a long flirtatious glance. She didn't seem at all anxious to take her place as the leader of Valley's

cheerleaders. Instead she looked eager to spend
more time with him. The romantic beach idea
seemed better and better.

"Let me get you another soda," Zack offered, and
slid out of the booth. He motioned for Screech to follow him.

"Yes, triple-oh-seven?" Screech whispered eagerly when they were a couple of tables away from
Brandi.

Zack donned a concerned expression. "I'm worried, Arnold . . . I mean, Screech."

"About Brandi?"

"About the game," Zack said. "We need to know
what the score is and what quarter they're in so we
don't get Brandi back there too soon."

"Hmm. Good point," Screech agreed. "After all,
she's a dangerous woman."

Zack and Screech both turned their heads to look
at Brandi as she sat waiting patiently in the booth.
She smiled and wiggled her fingers in a wave at them.

"Very dangerous," Zack repeated. He reached in
his jeans pocket and pulled out his car keys. "Here.
Take the Mustang and go find out how the game is
going. Then report back. I'll keep Brandi occupied
while you're gone."

"Check," Screech said. He glanced back at
Brandi. "Be careful, Zack."

"Don't worry. I will be," Zack promised, and
pushed his friend toward the door.

Before returning to the booth, he ordered two more colas from the waitress, all the while keeping Brandi in sight. It wouldn't do to lose her now, even if she didn't look at all eager to get lost. In fact, she looked just the opposite.

"Oh, I'm glad you got rid of Arnold," she purred when Zack slid into the booth next to her once again. Brandi leaned closer to him. "He's nice and all, but it's really hard for a girl to get to know a boy unless they're alone. Like they say, three's a crowd."

Zack glanced at the clock again, trying to guess how long it would take Screech to get to the game and back. How long it would be before he had his car once more and could be beach bound with the beautiful Brandi.

"Here," Brandi offered, taking the straw from his glass and sticking it next to hers in one of the fresh colas. "Share with me."

Any time, Zack thought. *Any time.*

Chapter 5

▲ ▼ ▲ ▼ ▲

"I'm really glad the team sent you to pick me up, Zack," Brandi said as, heads close together, they sipped on a single drink.

"Me, too," Zack agreed. It was almost a shame it would be both the first and the last time he saw her. Brandi was fun to be with, but she did go to Valley High. There were some flaws even great legs and gorgeous long blond hair couldn't cure.

"You see," Brandi continued, "I broke up with my boyfriend a couple of weeks ago, and it's been pretty lonely with no one special to do things with on the weekends."

"I know what you mean," Zack said with heart-felt sincerity. Things just hadn't been the same since Kelly had broken up with him. Being friends during the school day was fine, but when the moonlight glittered on the lapping waves at the beach, he really missed having a special girl to share the sight with.

"It isn't easy finding someone new, either," Brandi said. "It seems the more guys I meet, the more I know what I don't want, even if I'm not sure about what I do want."

Did Kelly feel that way? She was tired of his scams, especially when they involved other girls, but maybe, just maybe, she would find more she disliked in other guys than she did in him. There was hope yet!

But until Kelly realized she was better off with Zack Morris, there would always be babes like Brandi Jarrett to keep him company.

"You know," Brandi said in a breathy little voice. "You're such a good-looking guy, I can't believe you don't have a steady girlfriend."

Zack shrugged and tried to look modest. "You know how things go, Brandi. My heart was recently broken, but I'm sure the right girl could help it heal faster."

Brandi's lashes swept down over her eyes as she sipped daintily on her straw. "Maybe I could try to heal the pain, Zack."

"If you're willing, I suppose it's worth a try," Zack declared, and gave a tragic sigh. "I want to warn you ahead of time, though, it won't be easy."

"Oh, Zack," Brandi purred, and reached to brush

her fingers along his cheek. Instead, her elbow hit the twin straws and tipped the cola over on the table. In no time at all there was a bubbling cola river spilling ice cubes into her lap. With a shriek of surprise, Brandi jumped to her feet.

Zack jumped, too, far away from the threat of a soft-drink drenching.

"Oh, look at me!" Brandi wailed, dabbing at her damp cheerleading uniform with paper napkins. "I've got to wash this stickiness off before it stains! Which way is it to the restroom, Zack? This may take a while."

Forgetting he wasn't supposed to be familiar with the layout of the Max, Zack pointed Brandi in the right direction as a waitress hurried over with a rag to clean up the mess. Brandi hustled away, her attention entirely on her damp clothing.

When the booth was cola-free once more, Zack settled back to wait for her. He might not be able to flirt with her for a few minutes, but the time Brandi spent cleaning up was time well spent in Bayside's favor.

Zack was considering whether to have apple pie à la mode or a banana split with three kinds of syrup while he waited for her when Screech rushed up and dropped three dollars on the table.

"Bayside's ahead by seven points, and halftime is just ending," he announced, gasping for breath.

"Great! Then we don't have to delay Brandi

much longer," Zack said, and picked up the money Screech had dropped. "What's this for?"

"To pay the bill. What else?"

"We already paid it, Screech."

"We did?"

"We did."

"When?" A puzzled look contorted Screech's elastic face.

"After you ordered your second burger."

"Oh," Screech said, and sat down. "I wonder why Brandi told me you needed three dollars, then?"

Zack got a sick feeling in his stomach. "Brandi?" he croaked.

"Yeah. She was waiting for me outside when I drove up."

Oh no!

"She's really a nice girl, Zack," Screech went on. "Even if she does think my name is Arnold."

Zack felt really sick now. "What did you do with my keys?" he asked.

Screech's face lit up in a wide grin. "I left them in the car. Brandi's favorite song was playing on the radio, so I didn't want to turn it off and make her miss it."

Zack beat his head against the tabletop.

When he didn't look up, Screech lifted him by his hair. "Zack? You all right?"

"Yeah."

"Good," Screech said, and let go of Zack's hair. Zack's head smashed back against the table.

▲ ▼ ▲

It took half an hour for Zack and Screech to walk the distance to the football field. Long before they got there, they could hear the cheers of the fans.

"Maybe Brandi didn't drive your car to the game," Screech offered helpfully. "Maybe the Bayside Tigers are so far ahead of the Valley Mastodons even the new secret plays won't help them catch up."

"Maybe Slater won't rip me into tiny little pieces if they lose," Zack said.

"You don't have to worry about that, kemosabe," Screech assured him. "I *know* he will."

The sound of more cheering met them at the stands. Zack and Screech stumbled down to the sidelines just in time to see Valley trample past the Bayside team and score a touchdown as the clock ran out. The scoreboard lit up: Bayside 21, Valley 42. The game was over.

Across the field, Brandi Jarrett led the Valley cheerleaders in a wild victory cheer.

"A word with you, preppie," Slater growled. He looked even more threatening than usual in his football uniform. So did the other members of the team behind him. They all had black half-moons painted beneath their eyes and dirt and grass stains on their maroon-and-white uniforms. Zack gulped down a spurt of panic.

He backed up a step and ran into the Bayside

cheerleaders. Kelly and Lisa both stood in the front line, fists on their hips and disappointment in their eyes.

"Oh, Zack," Kelly cried. "Everything was going so well! What happened?"

Zack began inching away from the two angry groups of teens only to be cut off by a crowd of fans led by the hot dog vendor.

Screech stepped boldly up to his side. "It wasn't Zack's fault," he announced. "Brandi tricked us. She stole Zack's car and—"

"Come off it, preppie. You think we're going to believe that one? Stop hiding behind Screech and face the music."

"I'm not hiding behind Screech," Zack said from a position of debatable safety at Screech's back. "She *did* fool us and . . ."

Slater gathered a handful of Screech's shirt in his hand, pulled him forward in a threatening manner, and leaned over his shoulder to glare at Zack. "Are you telling me that a Valley girl pulled a scam on the Bayside scammeister?"

Zack swallowed loudly. "Er, yes," he said, his voice a bit squeaky. He closed his eyes, figuring it was better not to witness his own pulverizing.

"Oh, give me a break, you big galoots," a familiar voice said.

Zack opened one eye to see Brandi Jarrett pushing her way through the Bayside team. Even though they towered over her, the muscle-bound gorillas gave way before her determined stride.

"It's true. I did trick Zack." She tapped Slater on his shoulder pad. "Drop Arnold, too," she ordered.

"*Arnold?*" Slater echoed, but he did let Screech go.

"Arnold Benedict," Screech said, straightening his wildly patterned shirt and hooking his thumbs behind his glow-in-the-dark suspenders proudly. "That's my code name."

"Benedict Arnold, more like," Lisa murmured. "How could you let us all down? We were counting on you!"

"Like I said," Brandi repeated, "it isn't their fault. In fact, it was a very good plan." She linked arms with Zack and smiled up at him warmly. "You just didn't know your opponent well enough."

"Meaning the Valley team?" Slater growled.

"Meaning me," Brandi said. "You see, I knew you guys were from Bayside immediately. I've made it my business to check you all out, complete with photo surveillance. The members of the Valley camera club really enjoyed crawling around in bushes getting candid photographs of anyone connected with the football team. By the way, where is Jessie Spano? She's the only one of you I didn't see tonight."

"Oh, she's at . . . ," Screech began.

Lisa hit him over the head with one of her pom-poms.

"Very clever," Zack said. "But why go to all of that trouble?"

"Why not?" Brandi said. "You never know when you'll need to know the enemy."

Zack sighed deeply. "I don't think I like the sound of that."

Brandi giggled. "Oh, Zack. You'll never be my enemy." Her eyes sparkled with pleasure. "But you'll always be my opponent," she added, and tossed him the keys to his car. "Thanks for dinner, guys. See you later, Zack."

Feeling a bit dazed at the turn of events, Zack stared after Brandi as she strutted back across the field to a victory celebration with her own team.

"Now what do you think she meant by that?" Slater asked.

Just before she reached the Valley side of the field, Brandi spun around and threw kisses to the Bayside football players. Some of them looked a little dreamy eyed.

Zack didn't blame them. "I have no idea," he said. "But I think I'm looking forward to finding out."

Chapter 6

▲ ▼ ▲ ▼ ▲

Nicki Kapowski swung through the door of Kelly's room and plopped down on her sister's bed. "You really going out with this new guy?" Nicki asked, her voice clearly indicating she found the idea mind-boggling. Nicki had had a major crush on Zack. And even though she knew they had broken up, she couldn't believe Kelly would even consider dating someone else.

Kelly checked the time. It was almost nine-thirty, and Austin would be knocking on the door soon. She'd rushed home from the football game, barely dropping the news to her parents that Bayside had gone down in defeat before barreling up the stairs to her room to take a quick shower and change. Now she watched Nicki's reflection in the mirror as she quickly brushed her hair. "Of course I am. He called and asked me out and I accepted."

"Yeah, but you don't know him from Adam," Nicki said.

"Sure I do," Kelly insisted. "Adam Weatherwax already has a bald spot, and he's got ears as big as Dumbo's." Adam was a teenager who lived two doors away and played the tuba in the Bayside marching band. He'd worshiped Kelly for years.

Who had time to worry about him, though? Her date would be arriving any minute! Kelly swept her hair up on one side with a comb and let the rest cascade down her back. "Austin Vogel doesn't look anything like Adam," she assured her sister.

Nicki gave her a disgusted look. "I meant, Austin is a complete stranger. Anyway, how do you know what he looks like?"

"His mother showed me a picture of him," Kelly explained patiently. She stepped back a bit from the mirror and carefully considered her reflection. The pink miniskirt was one of her favorites and looked great with the pink, green, orange, and yellow Hawaiian-print shirt she'd borrowed from her mother for the occasion. Now, what earrings should she wear?

Nicki switched her position, twisting her long legs into a lotus position. "So what's he look like?" she demanded.

"Hmm? What's who look like?" Kelly asked as she sorted through her jewelry box. Gold hoops? No, too much. Pearl studs? Too formal.

Nicki rolled her eyes. "Earth to Kelly! What's this Austin guy look like?"

"Oh." Kelly wrinkled her nose in thought. Why was it that whenever she was trying to get ready in a hurry, one of her brothers or sisters decided to play twenty questions? Didn't they realize how important each decision she had to make was? She'd just have to let Lisa give them her "The Importance of Completing the Fashion Picture" talk.

"Well, Austin's got blond hair and blue eyes and he's in college," she said, and continued her search for the perfect earrings.

Nicki propped an elbow on her knee and her chin in the palm of her hand. "College, huh. Does that mean he shaves?"

"I suppose so."

"Hmm," Nicki murmured. "Interesting. What if he doesn't: Would you still like him?"

"I suppose so. I don't know yet. This is our first date. Why all the questions? And have you seen my new dangle earrings?"

"Oh, you mean these?" Nicki held up a pair of earrings. The pink plastic studs dripped icicles of green, orange, and yellow. "I was hoping to borrow Mom's blouse first, and these go great with it. And I only asked about your blind date because there's a guy downstairs waiting for you."

"*What!*" Kelly flew to the mirror for a last check

of her appearance as she hastily fastened the wildly colored earrings in place. "Why didn't you tell me?" She stepped into a pair of pink flats.

"Don't worry. He's being entertained," Nicki soothed. "I've got Billy staring him down." Billy was their three-year-old brother. Staring at strangers was something he excelled at.

"Oh, and Kel?"

Kelly paused at the door wondering what parting words of wisdom her sister could possibly give.

"This Austin guy's got a mustache. A funny looking one. Personally," Nicki said, "I think I'd rather be seen with Adam Weatherwax."

▲   ▼   ▲

Austin had more than just a mustache, Kelly realized when she reached the living room. He was attempting to grow a beard. His face bristled with short blond spikes that looked undernourished against his pale skin.

Billy sat on the floor in front of Austin, his thumb in his mouth, his favorite stuffed animal in his arms, his gaze nearly unblinking as he watched the young man seated on the sofa.

Kelly wasn't surprised when Austin jumped eagerly to his feet as she entered the room. Billy's stare had driven lots of visitors nuts.

"Kelly?" Austin croaked hopefully. His eyes dipped to take in her appearance. A pleased smile curved his lips. Her sister Nicki had no taste where boys were concerned, Kelly decided, because, even with his scruffy beard, this guy was really super delicious looking.

"Hi," he said in a pleasant-sounding deep voice. "I'm Austin Vogel." He held out his hand.

He was as tall as Zack or Slater, but his shoulders were a bit stooped. Probably from bending over all those psychology books at the university, Kelly decided. Neither Zack nor Slater cared much for studying. They were only interested in having fun. Meeting a guy who was already seriously working toward his future profession was a nice change.

Kelly nudged Billy with her foot, giving him the signal to find someone else to stare at. She shook Austin's hand as Billy ran out of the room, his thumb still in his mouth. "It's nice to meet you."

"Hey, well," Austin said, and gave her a nervous grin. "You ready to go to that school dance?" he asked.

Kelly's smile faded. She sighed. "I'd rather do something else if you don't mind. It would be like going to a funeral since Bayside lost."

"I know," Austin said, his blue eyes filled with understanding. "I was at the game."

Kelly's mouth nearly dropped open in surprise. "You were?" she gasped.

"Sure. Why not?" He shrugged. The movement was poetry in motion, so smooth, so debonair, so manly.

"But I thought you told me you didn't go to high school around here," Kelly said.

Austin shoved his hands in the pockets of his jeans and gave her a sheepish look. It was enough to melt any girl's heart. "I didn't, but I still like football games, even if I don't know anybody on either of the teams," he said. "By the way, you lead some great cheers."

"Thanks. But they weren't good enough," Kelly said sadly. "I thought maybe you'd be visiting friends while you're in Palisades."

Austin shrugged again. "Well, I would if there were any to visit. Most everybody I used to hang around with is away at college, and they come home only during the holidays. You'll have the same problem once you graduate, Kelly, and your friends all go to different schools."

"Oh, that's so sad, Austin," Kelly murmured, and touched his arm in sympathy.

He covered her hand with one of his and smiled down into her eyes. "It's not that bad. Besides, it gives me a chance to make new friends. Especially beautiful girls like you, Kelly."

He had a nice smile. She was glad his beard hadn't grown enough to hide it yet.

"So, how about a movie instead?" Austin suggested. "There's a great retrospective being shown at the Palace Theater. It's a 1940s romantic comedy."

A romantic comedy? That was sure a far cry from

the type of movies Zack had always taken her to see. They usually involved car chases or renegade robots.

"I'd love to see it," Kelly told him.

"Great," Austin said, and dropped his arm around her shoulder as they walked out to his car.

Kelly sighed happily. Perhaps blind dates weren't so bad after all.

▲　▼　▲

Zack pulled up in front of Slater's house and waited for his friend to hop out, gym bag in hand.

"Did you ever decide who to take to the dance?" Zack asked casually. Not that it was going to be much fun to attend after that game. He was just happy the team had gone off to the showers instead of deciding to practice a Mexican hat dance using him as the hat.

"Oh yeah, I had a plan," Slater said. "I was going to go with whatever girl hurled herself into my arms after we made the winning touchdown."

"Whoops! So what happens now?"

Slater grinned, his deep dimples flashing. "Plan B, that's what. I'm going over to Jessie's Green Teens meeting. They always run late. And there are a lot of good-looking but lonely girls at those meetings."

"Not to mention Jessie," Zack added.

"We're just friends, preppie, like you and Kelly are," Slater said.

"Which makes us both major dweebs to have lost them," Zack said.

"You got it," Slater agreed. "See you later, preppie. Oh, by the way. The team told me to tell you they wish you sweet dreams."

Well, that certainly guaranteed he'd have night-mares! Probably about being trampled by buffalos wearing cleats, Zack mused as he drove off. He'd already taken Screech home, delaying the moment when he had to meet the *nice* girl his mother had fixed him up with for the dance. Not that he had any intention of making an appearance in the Bayside gym anytime soon. In fact, the farther away from the place he could get, the safer he would be!

There was no putting off the inevitable, though. He just had to keep reminding himself that his blind date drove a Ferrari. As long as she handed him the keys, she could look like Barney Rubble.

Well, almost. Even he had standards.

There was no Ferrari in front of his parents' house when he got home, which meant that his blind date was late. It was after nine-thirty. Maybe she wasn't coming. Zack couldn't decide if that bothered him or not.

It might be smarter to take a page from Slater's book and crash the Green Teens meeting. He'd seen some super babes among Jessie's fellow protesters when they'd marched a few months ago to save the whales. His muscle-bound friend had come up with a surprisingly brilliant move. Would he get very far, though, with Jessie there tossing her zingers around about the small amount of gray matter in a

Neanderthal's head? At least Zack Morris had a reputation as a thinking man.

Or he had until tonight.

Zack parked his car and was swinging himself over the driver's door when a sleek red sports car pulled up to the curb. The sound of the motor was like a leopard's purr, deep and rumbling. The kind of sound that made a boy's heart perform back flips with joy.

The license plate was white with silver etched mountains—a Nevada plate.

The engine died with a quiet sigh. The driver's-side door swung open, and a cowboy boot and a long, shapely female leg swung out, stepping onto the pavement. It was followed by a knockout girl dressed in a short leather skirt and a fringed bolero top. She wore her long platinum blond hair in a ponytail that swished from side to side as she moved.

The girl gave the car door a push with her hip and turned with a coy smile.

"Why the surprised look, Zack? I told you I'd see you soon," Brandi Jarrett purred.

Chapter 7

▲ ▼ ▲ ▼ ▲

Everyone at the Green Teens meeting was really excited about the new crusade Sequoia and Evergreen had brought to their attention. Although she had left the talking to her brother earlier, the green-haired girl had turned out to be very knowledgeable and not nearly as weird in personality as she was in looks. Shelly whispered to Jessie that she thought Evergreen had chosen to color her hair just to get people's attention.

If that was the plan, she certainly was successful, Jessie thought as she watched Evergreen pass out flyers and answer questions.

Jessie stood off to the side and watched. She wondered when she would learn why Sequoia had signaled her *not* to be one of the volunteers. It seemed very strange, considering how involved he was in the project.

Unless he hadn't wanted to be around her.

What if he really didn't want to date her? What if his interest in her had all been in Shelly's head? She had to talk to Shelly.

Jessie looked around for her friend only to see Slater swing through the doors of the community room and look around.

Oh no! Was he looking for her?

Well, that could be good and it could be bad. If Sequoia wasn't interested in her, she wouldn't look like she'd been stood up if she left with Slater. But if Sequoia was interested and Slater's presence discouraged him from going out with her . . . oh, what was a girl to do?

Jessie stared hard at Slater, willing him to leave. Instead, he spotted her in the crowd and strolled over to her side.

"Greetings, momma. How's things?" he asked.

Jessie frowned at him. "What are you doing here? Shouldn't you be at the victory dance?"

"Naw. It's being held at Valley, and I didn't feel like going," Slater said.

"You lost? What happened to Zack's plan?"

"Zack happened to it," Slater answered. His eyes skimmed over the crowd, then returned to rest on a couple of girls giggling on the opposite side of the room.

Jessie touched his arm. "I'm sorry Bayside lost."

He shrugged. "There'll be other games. Hey, tell me who the two redheads are. I don't think I've ever seen them at any of your marches."

Redheads? "You mean you didn't come here to see me?" Jessie demanded.

"Heck, no. I can see you anytime. I came to pick up girls. So who are they? I think they like me." When the redheads wiggled their fingers at him, Slater returned the wave and gave the giggling girls a wide grin, flashing his devastatingly cute dimples.

He was just looking for girls? Jessie fumed. Well, what did she expect from the muscle-bound idiot? Slater had a one-track mind when it came to girls, and nothing she could do was going to derail it!

"You mean the twins?" Jessie asked, keeping her voice casual.

Slater's dark eyes brightened. "Twins!"

"Kimberly and Courtney Kilgore."

"Which is which?"

Jessie tossed her curly brown hair over her shoulder in an I-don't-care gesture. "I have no idea."

"Great!" Slater said enthusiastically. "Guess I'll go find out. See you later, momma."

Boys! There was no living with them.

Sequoia excused himself from a group of kids and walked directly toward Jessie. She sighed. Thank goodness there was no living without them, either.

"I'm sorry I kept you, Jessie," Sequoia said in his

rich, deep voice. It made her toes want to curl in pleasure. "Shelly said something about a dance? I've got to confess, I'm not too light on my toes." He grinned. "Or anybody else's, I've been told."

"That's all right. I don't really feel like dancing, either. I'd rather hear more about what Desert Beauty is doing and how you found out so much about them. You haven't been in Palisades long, have you?" Jessie asked.

"Long enough," Sequoia said, and brushed back his long, bark-colored hair. "How about if we go someplace quiet, then? I'd like to learn more about you, Jessie."

Jessie glowed deep down inside. He wanted to know more about her! Oh, but not as much as she wanted to know about him.

"It sounds kind of corny and romantic," she said, "but there's a beautiful place called Smuggler's Cove. It's a secluded, crescent-shaped beach."

He smiled softly and touched a lock of her hair gently with the backs of his fingers. "I don't think that sounds corny at all. And I happen to be a sucker for romantic places."

"I'll drive," Jessie offered. She was a little surprised when Sequoia didn't insist on driving himself. But then he was nothing like Slater. Sequoia was secure enough about himself to let a girl be his equal. He didn't need the macho act other guys put on.

Oh, wasn't it great to finally meet a guy like him?

Good thing Shelly had talked her into going out with him. This was going to be the experience of a life-time!

▲   ▼   ▲

Zack was in heaven. He leaned back into the Ferrari's bucket seat and let his arm rest on the steering wheel, waiting for the light to change. Not only was he in a boss car, but one of the most gorgeous girls in the world was seated at his side. Life just didn't get any better than this.

"So," he said suavely, "where do you want to go?"

Brandi gave him a twinkling smile. "The Bayside dance?" she suggested.

Remembering the rabid look in the team's eyes, Zack shook his head. "I don't think so. You want to try Valley's?"

"Not particularly," Brandi said. "Let's face it, Zack. It isn't cool to date someone from a rival school."

He wasn't cool enough? *Pardon me? Does she know who she is talking to?*

"I like to live dangerously, though," Brandi added. "That's why I coaxed Daddy into letting me drive the Ferrari tonight. And since you're a really cute guy, I think I'll keep you for a while."

That was a relief.

The light changed. The sports car hummed beneath Zack's hands as he eased it into gear and cruised down the street. "I was really impressed with the way you scammed me at the Max tonight," he said.

Brandi giggled. "At least you aren't mad at me. I had fun tricking you. You were so gullible."

Zack swallowed. He didn't like the sound of that much. It made it seem like he was losing his touch.

"Of course, I learned from a master scammer," Brandi confessed. "Daddy has always talked his way either out of or into anything he wanted."

"Really?" Now this sounded interesting. He'd always been afraid that scamming was something a teenager outgrew, and he'd never wanted to do that. He liked it too much! "Tell me something your dad scammed."

Brandi twisted in her seat so that she was nearly facing him. Zack couldn't help himself from grabbing a long look at her shapely bare legs. This was turning into one great night.

"First I have to swear you to secrecy," Brandi insisted. "Your sacred word as a scammeister."

Zack mimed buttoning his lip.

"All right. Daddy says this rates the Nobel prize for most daring scam. He targeted the job of vice president at Inspirations, Inc. You know, the local computer animation company?"

Zack had heard his father mention the innovative company. Following in the tradition of special effects pioneered in moviemaking, Inspirations had used the same technology to make spectacular advertising promotions and sales materials for many of Palisades' businesses.

"Daddy lacked most of the qualifications for a management job. He never finished college, although everyone thinks he did. And he isn't mathematical at all, so trying to bluff his way into a place where everyone else was either an engineering nerd or a computer geek took more guts than if he'd been running for president."

"I can imagine!" Zack said, awed at the scope of Brandon Jarrett's master scam. "Had he been a vice president anywhere else?"

Brandi smiled proudly. "Nope. But Daddy's a gambler, and he liked the stakes."

"Did he get the job?"

"Absolutely! Not only that, but an unlimited expense account and the whole southwestern sales district." She was beaming now. "There isn't another man like my dad."

Zack could believe it. "I'd like to shake his hand," he said with heartfelt wonder.

"Okay!" Brandi shouted. "Let's do it, then. Daddy is throwing a party at our house, and he said we were more than welcome to join in the fun." She tossed her head so that her long blond ponytail swished over her shoulder. "I think you know the way, don't you, Zack?"

▲   ▼   ▲

Kelly let Austin open the front door of the

Kapowski house for her. He was such a gentleman! Not that Zack wasn't, but because they'd grown up together, Zack took her for granted.

"I'm glad you suggested that movie, Austin," she said softly. "I really enjoyed it."

He grinned down at her. "I had fun, too. Although I don't usually say this, I'm really glad my mother was in her matchmaking mood the day she met you at the mall."

"Yeah, me too," Kelly agreed. She wished their date weren't already over. This night could go on forever as far as she was concerned.

"Hey, would you like a soda before you go?" she offered.

Beneath his scrawny mustache, Austin's lips curved in a smile of acceptance.

"Follow me, then," Kelly instructed. "The kitchen is this way. Lucky for you it isn't exactly LAX at this time of night. Sounds like only my parents are there right now."

She was halfway down the hall when Austin grabbed her arm and pulled her to a stop.

"*Shh*," he cautioned. "This might not be a good time to interrupt them."

"Oh, they won't mind. In fact, I know they'd like to meet you."

Austin shook his head. "You don't understand," he said softly. "It sounds like they are arguing."

Arguing? Her parents? They rarely did that.

Money was tight, but between her dad's job as a fore-man and her mother's job as a legal secretary, the Kapowskis got by. There might be seven kids in the family, but there were enough older children to supply handy baby-sitters for the younger ones when necessary. There were some things they all had to do without, but love wasn't one of those things.

"Listen," Austin urged.

Feeling like she was invading her parents' privacy, Kelly listened.

"I don't agree with that at all," her mother said. "Your sister already has three young children. It would be impossible for her to give Billy the affection and attention that he needs. I think he should go to my brother's house instead."

"But he lives in Toledo, and he told you the company he works for might close," Mr. Kapowski insisted.

"Well, we've got to make up our minds about this and what we should arrange for the other children!" Mrs. Kapowski cried. "I don't like breaking them up, but I really don't see any other option. We have to decide this now."

What were her parents talking about? Why were they planning to send little Billy to live with someone else? Why did the family have to be broken up?

Quietly, Austin drew Kelly back down the hall to the front door. "I'm so sorry, Kelly."

"I'm sorry, too, Austin. I don't know what is going on but—"

"Oh, I do," he said. "It's easy to understand once you have been trained to recognize it."

"What is?" Kelly asked, still puzzled over what she had overheard.

Austin took her hand and held it between his. The look in his eyes was kind as he bent over her. "Kelly, your parents are getting a divorce."

"A divorce?" Kelly whispered, praying she had heard him wrong.

"Remember, my mother is a family counselor and I'm going into the field myself. I've been studying a good deal, and from what I just heard, it sounds like your parents have both been talking to lawyers and are in the final stages of divorce proceedings. They're now making arrangements for the care of their children," Austin said.

They couldn't be! They were such a happy family! And if her parents really were getting a divorce, how had they kept it a secret from her for so long? How could she not have seen signs that they *weren't* happy together?

"Oh, Austin, what am I going to do?" Kelly murmured.

He patted her shoulder. "Don't worry. I'll help you all I can, Kelly. You can pick my brain if you'd like."

He grinned as if he'd made a joke, but Kelly didn't feel the least bit like laughing. How could she have been so blind?

"How about if I pick you up tomorrow morning and take you to the beach? You can ask me any questions you might have. I'll be glad to answer them," Austin said.

What a horribly self-centered daughter she had been, Kelly moaned silently. She had been so involved with her own life, first in breaking up with Zack, then with her short romance with Slater, she never realized there was tension in her own home.

"Kelly?" Austin asked.

"Oh! Yes, I'd like to meet you tomorrow, Austin," she answered.

"I'm glad," he said, and leaned forward to kiss her.

Her mind on the pending disaster, Kelly didn't even notice his intention and turned away.

Austin had to catch his balance quickly against the wall.

"Good-night," he called as he closed the front door behind him.

It had been a good night for a little while, Kelly admitted to herself. But between the football game and her parents' problems, it was ending up to be one of the worst nights of her life!

Chapter 8

▲ ▼ ▲ ▼ ▲

The area of town where the Jarretts lived looked a lot different than it had earlier that evening when he and Screech had . . . er . . . kidnapped Brandi, Zack realized. Then the neighborhood had seemed deserted, it had been so quiet. Now expensive cars lined the street, leaving only a narrow spot free near the front of the house. It looked big enough for Denny Vane's wheezing old VW Bug but not spacious enough for the sleek, red Ferrari.

"Oh, good!" Brandi cried. "Somebody left us a parking space!"

Zack swallowed loudly, sweat breaking out on his forehead just at the thought of trying to parallel park the Ferrari into the narrow space without scratching the paint job. Once the impossible mission was completed successfully, he breathed a lot easier.

The party was in full swing. Lights glowed in the windows of every room, and music and laughter echoed from behind the house.

"Daddy's probably out back by the pool," Brandi said as she climbed out of the low-slung car. "I'd introduce you around to some of the guests, but I know only a few of these people."

"You forget. I already know Sheila," Zack pointed out. "She works with my mom."

Brandi tossed her head. "Oh, she's history. She won't be here tonight."

Zack felt confused. "But isn't she the one who fixed us up?"

"Yeah. So?"

"I thought she and your dad were seeing each other," Zack said.

"They were," Brandi agreed. "But I didn't care much for her, so I put an end to that little romance. Poor Sheila. She really didn't have a chance. Once I put my mind to something, I always get my way."

Brandi breezed into the house and through a series of crowded rooms. She ignored the guests, even the ones who looked up with a smile of recognition on their faces. Her actions seemed impolite to Zack. His parents had drummed into him the necessity of always chatting pleasantly for a few moments with people he knew, especially the Morrises' friends and business associates. Brandi's rudeness made him a little uneasy.

Since he didn't know any of the guests, there wasn't much Zack could do but trail in Brandi's wake.

"Did your dad really break up with Sheila just because you wanted him to?" he asked.

Brandi tossed an amused look over her shoulder. "Don't be ridiculous. I made it so that Sheila broke it off with him. It was so simple."

She paused in the doorway and scanned the guests in the patio area looking for her father. "Have you ever noticed how gullible some people are? You can pull one scam after another on them, and they never catch on."

Zack thought about Mr. Belding, the principal at Bayside High. He'd pulled so many scams on Mr. Belding, and gotten caught, that being in detention at the end of the school day felt as normal to him as going home did. The thing was, he really liked Mr. Belding. He just couldn't help himself when an opportunity to scam came along.

It didn't sound like Brandi had cared much for Sheila. Zack couldn't understand why. Sheila was pretty, smart, and a very nice lady.

"Get this," Brandi said, her voice pitched low so that only he could hear. "Sheila called a couple of days ago and asked to leave a message for Dad. I acted like I wasn't sure who she was and called her Susan. And I then acted like I was really embarrassed to get her name wrong. I tried to explain the mistake by saying Susan had eaten dinner with us the night before and that Dad was expecting a call from her. The next time Daddy phoned Sheila, she slammed the receiver down without even talking to him."

Brandi smiled proudly. "Clever, huh?"

Zack thought it had been mean rather than clever. But then, he'd always thought he was being clever when he scammed Kelly. She had always thought he was doing some good deed when all he'd been doing was hanging out with a different girl. Now he knew he hadn't been clever, he'd been stupid. Real stupid.

"Oh, there's Daddy," Brandi cried, and weaving her fingers through Zack's, drew him to poolside.

Brandon Jarrett's smile of greeting was wide as he shook Zack's hand after Brandi introduced them. "So you're the young man who tripped my little girl up tonight," he said. He was standing near a portable bar. A man in a white shirt, black vest, and red bow tie stood behind it mixing drinks. Mr. Jarrett ordered two colas.

"I think you've got that wrong, sir," Zack replied as Brandi's father handed him one of the sodas. "Your daughter tricked *me* in the end."

"Sounds to me like you're a pretty evenly matched pair," Mr. Jarrett declared.

Brandi snuggled closer to Zack. "I think so, too," she said, and smiled up at him. "I sure wish we weren't leaving tomorrow morning. It would be a lot more fun to spend time with Zack this weekend than it will be to go visit Susan."

Zack nearly choked on his cola. Susan? Mr. Jarrett really did have another girlfriend? Maybe his mother's friend Sheila was better off not dating this guy.

"I don't think your Aunt Susan can live without her Ferrari much longer," Brandi's father said. "If she hadn't been in such a hurry to get back to Nevada, you wouldn't have been able to drive the car this long."

"Oh, well," Brandi sighed. "You see, Zack, Susan is a very talented dancer. She used to have a job on a cruise ship and left her car with us while she was gone. Then she landed a spot in a show in Las Vegas and hopped the next plane out of here."

"Hey! That's awesome!" Zack declared, impressed. "So you're going to Vegas tomorrow?"

"Unfortunately," Brandi admitted. "I'm not looking forward to it much. That five-hour drive across the desert is about the most boring thing in the world."

"You'd be bored driving a Ferrari?" Zack asked in shock.

Brandi giggled. "Well, not totally. It would be better if I didn't have to drive alone, though." She turned to her father, pouting a bit in an effort to get her own way. "You're sure you can't get out of that lunch meeting?"

Mr. Jarrett looked a bit sad. "Sorry, pumpkin.

Business is business. I'd much rather be with you than on that early morning flight. But we'll be together again by dinner."

"Oh, all right," Brandi said, although she didn't sound happy.

"Although," Mr. Jarrett murmured thoughtfully. He studied Zack. "Have you ever been to Las Vegas, young man?"

Zack did choke on his soft drink this time. "No, sir."

"I really hate to have my daughter drive all that way by herself," Mr. Jarrett said. "There's some pretty desolate landscape between Palisades and Vegas. Would you be interested in being her codriver on the trip?"

"Would I!" Zack shouted excitedly. What a weekend! Cruising for five glorious hours behind the wheel of that beautiful sports car with the gorgeous Brandi at his side. And then the glitter and excitement of Las Vegas at the end of the drive . . .

The bubble burst when he remembered there was a slight complication to achieving the perfect weekend.

"Er . . . I'd love to go, but I don't think my parents will let me," Zack said.

Mr. Jarrett grinned. He put a firm hand on Zack's shoulder. "Why don't you let me talk to them, my boy. I'll see what I can do."

Brandi touched her glass of soda to Zack's.

"Here's to our trip tomorrow," she said. "It should be really fun now."

Zack didn't feel as confident as Brandi and her dad. "Don't count on it. You don't know my parents," he warned.

Brandi grinned widely. "And you don't know my daddy," she said.

▲ ▼ ▲

The moonlight glistened on the waves as they rolled onto the shore. Jessie leaned back on her elbows in the sand watching the water inch toward her, then retreat down the beach again. A soft, cool breeze wafted inshore from the Pacific Ocean, playfully teasing her curly brown hair.

Sequoia was seated at her side, but rather than relax and enjoy the beauty of Smuggler's Cove, he leaned forward, his arms linked around his drawn-up legs.

"So you see," he said, "if the desert plants are completely removed, the ecology of the area will be destroyed. With mature plant life gone, the native birds, mammals, and reptiles will die out as well. When the rains come, there will be nothing to prevent the soil from being washed away, making it impossible for any new plants to grow. The cycle will be completely destroyed. In a very short time the desert east of Palisades will be as barren as a moonscape."

Jessie could tell he was upset about the pending

disaster from the sound of his deep voice.

"It won't happen," she assured him. "You're new to this Green Teens chapter but believe me, we are an extremely diligent group. The kids who volunteered tonight are very efficient when it comes to organizing protests and getting the public involved."

Sequoia leaned back and stretched out next to her. Rolling on his side to face her, he caught a lock of Jessie's hair and twisted it around his finger. "They may very well be," he murmured. "But I've heard that you're the most dedicated and serious Green Teen in Palisades. That's why I wanted to see you outside of the meeting."

"Really?" Jessie felt flattered. "I don't think I'm any more devoted to our cause than any of the others. We all work hard."

He continued to play with the lock of her hair. "The fact that you have beauty as well as brains is a real turn-on, Jessie."

Wow!

"You're really good-looking, too, Sequoia," she said. There wasn't enough moonlight to see much of his expression, but Jessie had a feeling that if she could see him clearly, she'd know that he wanted to kiss her.

She sure wanted to kiss him.

"I'm glad I took Shelly's advice and made the effort to get to know you better," Sequoia said. "It was hard to believe everything she said about you.

Now that I've spent some time with you, I see that it's all true." He released the stray lock of hair and brushed his fingers across her lips in a feather-light touch.

Jessie's heart started beating faster. He was going to kiss her!

"Help me stop Desert Beauty, Jessie Spano," Sequoia whispered softly.

"I'll do everything I can," Jessie promised.

"Do you mean that?"

"Absolutely," Jessie breathed, and closed her eyes. He was going to kiss her now. She was sure of it.

But he didn't.

Sequoia got to his feet and reached down a hand to help Jessie up. "Let's walk," he said.

Okay. Strolling along the beach with the moonlight smiling down on them and the soft sound of the surf making music in their ears was romantic. Jessie had no objection to that. He'd hold her hand, and when the time was right he'd draw her close and kiss her.

Sequoia didn't hold her hand. Instead he started walking quickly down the beach. Jessie had to almost run through the sand to keep up with his long strides.

"What I'm about to tell you is top secret, Jessie. And dangerous."

"I won't tell a soul," Jessie vowed.

"Even if you were tortured?"

Jessie gulped. *"Tortured?"*

Sequoia chuckled. "I was joking."

"Oh."

"But only about the torture," he said. "Have you ever heard of a group called the Green Gremlins?"

"You mean like the little creatures in those monster movies?" Jessie asked.

"Not exactly. You do know what a gremlin is, don't you?"

"Sure," Jessie assured him. "Ah, but just in case, why don't you tell me what you mean."

Sequoia stopped and stared out at the ocean. "It's a term aircraft mechanics use to describe a troublesome mechanical problem, something that messes up the system and keeps it from working as planned," he explained.

"Exactly," Jessie said, a bit relieved that he wasn't talking about ugly little creatures.

"The Green Gremlins do just that."

Jessie nodded, although she couldn't figure out what airplanes had to do with Desert Beauty's plan to turn the desert into desolation.

"We're a secret subgroup within Green Teens," Sequoia said. "I founded it with my sister."

It was nice to hear that Sequoia exercised equality of the sexes in Green Gremlins. Still, Jessie wondered why he was telling her about the group.

"You know how slowly matters are attended to by officials," Sequoia continued. "All that red tape drags."

"Yeah, it's really lame," Jessie agreed. "I remember when—"

"The Green Gremlins cut through the red tape," Sequoia said, not letting her finish.

Feeling very confused, Jessie stared at him. With Sequoia's profile outlined by the starlit sky, Jessie didn't think there was another guy in all of Palisades who was as handsome. Now, if he would just look at her with as much pleasure as he did the ocean, this evening would be perfect.

"The Green Gremlins don't form committees, carry signs, or march," Sequoia told her. "We act immediately to stop the destruction of the world."

"You do?"

Sequoia turned to Jessie. "It is a special honor to be asked to join us." His hands cupped her face, tipping it up to his. "I want you to join us, Jessie. Join me. Become one of the Green Gremlins."

Her heart filled with pride. This was indeed a special honor. So that was why he hadn't wanted her to be on the committee formed at the meeting earlier. He'd had a reason. A wonderful, secret reason.

"Yes," Jessie breathed happily. "Oh yes. I'd love to be a Green Gremlin, Sequoia."

Chapter 9

▲ ▼ ▲ ▼ ▲

It was just a few minutes after ten o'clock on Saturday morning when the gorgeous red Ferrari arrived in front of the Morris house. Zack bounded out the front door, a duffle bag of clothes in his hand, still half afraid that he was dreaming. The car was real though, the purr of its motor music to his ears. And his parents were both smiling and waving in the doorway, telling him to have a good time. Just in case, Zack pinched himself to make sure he was awake.

Brandi had been right. Her dad was amazing. He'd come back to Zack's house the night before and had personally asked Mr. and Mrs. Morris for a big favor. That was the way he'd phrased it. He'd explained to them that business made it impossible for him to accompany Brandi and that, while their housekeeper had originally planned to go along, she'd been called away when her daughter gave birth to her first baby. He would worry about Brandi if she were driving alone, Mr. Jarrett had said. If his sister hadn't needed her car back immediately, he would have put the trip off. As it was, his hands were tied. If Zack could go with Brandi, it would ease his mind.

Zack had stood by, watching in amazement as his parents had fallen under Mr. Jarrett's spell. He'd thought he was hearing things when they gave permission for him to go with Brandi on the long drive to Las Vegas.

Life seemed pretty perfect as he waved them a quick good-bye and slid into the Ferrari next to Brandi.

Brandi drove the first leg of the trip, weaving her way from one freeway system to another until they were headed directly east to Nevada.

"Heaven," Zack sighed as he sprawled, at ease in the passenger seat. "Pure heaven."

Brandi giggled. "Do you mean the car, the trip, or being with me?"

"All of the above," Zack said.

"I thought we'd stop at Barstow for lunch," she said.

"Sounds great to me." Zack closed his eyes in ecstasy, letting the dry, warm wind whip at his hair as they sped along. "I feel almost guilty to be having this much fun while your housekeeper is missing out on a great trip."

"Oh, we don't have a housekeeper," Brandi said.

Zack's eyes popped open. "You don't have a housekeeper? Then who was it that went off to see the new baby?"

Brandi shrugged. "Search me."

"But your father told my parents that . . ."

Brandi tossed him a knowing smile. "He made it up," she said. "Would your mom and dad have let you go if he hadn't added that sappy touch? I think not."

Zack was stunned. Mr. Jarrett had lied to his parents?

"What's it matter?" Brandi asked. "You wanted to come with me, and here you are. More importantly, I wanted you to come along. Daddy only did what was necessary to give me what I wanted."

"But . . ."

"Come off it, Zack. How many times have you scammed your parents?"

The list was too long to even think about. But that was different. He was their son. It was expected that he try to pull a few fast ones on them. And since they usually caught him at it, the scales evened out. But to have Mr. Jarrett scam them was an entirely different matter. Zack wasn't sure how he felt about it.

"I'm just surprised," he said. "Your dad sounded so . . . so *truthful* about it. I suppose you're going to tell me now that your Aunt Susan isn't real either."

Brandi grinned. "Almost. She isn't Daddy's sister or my real aunt. He just calls her that. She's an old friend. Daddy invited her to stay with us, but Susan thinks life in Palisades is too quiet. So do I. There isn't enough to do there."

Not enough to do in Palisades? Was she kidding? There was the beach! If a boy didn't want to surf or play volleyball, he could always watch the girls in bikinis.

"Why the frown, Zack? You worried you'll get in trouble if your parents find out Daddy told them a tall tale?"

He was, but there was no way he was going to let her know that. Zack stretched his arm out along the back of the seat, trying to at least look relaxed and cool. "Heck, no. It isn't like I knew about it. So, you've been to Las Vegas before?"

"We used to live there. In fact, we still have a condo near the Strip. The view is fantastic, and the location is really convenient to places like the MGM theme park."

Zack tried to regain his earlier enthusiasm. This was a once in a lifetime trip, he told himself. And he hadn't been the one to pull the scam to make it possible. Had he felt this bad when he conned Mr. Belding into chaperoning the gang on a trip to the mountains? No. So why the nagging conscience now?

"There's Barstow," Brandi announced. "After lunch, why don't you drive the rest of the way?"

Zack's worries evaporated. There was nothing like being behind the wheel of a truly awesome car to take a boy's mind off heavier things. Next to this, everything else seemed insignificant.

▲   ▼   ▲

Although Kelly watched her parents carefully all through breakfast, she could find nothing different about the way they treated each other. Had she imagined the discussion she'd overheard? Had it all been a bad dream?

"Did you have a nice time with Austin last night?" her mother asked cheerfully.

"Mmm," Kelly mumbled.

"Did you go to the dance?"

"No. We decided on a movie instead."

"I'm sorry we didn't get to meet him," her father said with a teasing grin. "Have to keep my eye on these college guys."

If her parents were having problems, they certainly hid them well from her and her brothers and sisters. Kelly cornered her brother Kyle before he left for a game of touch football, but he thought she was nuts when she asked him if he had noticed any sign of their parents having problems. "Come off it, Kel. Mom and Dad?" Kyle demanded. "No way."

Perhaps Austin was wrong. She sure hoped he was.

It was a beautiful day, which lifted Kelly's spirits. The sun was bright, the air was warm, and the sky was a clear blue. It was perfect weather for a day at the beach. Kelly chose her cutest bikini to wear and pulled on loose-fitting shorts and an oversized T-shirt. Twisting her hair up into a ponytail, she slipped into sandals and was ready when Austin rang the doorbell.

He looked even more gorgeous with the sun haloing his hair. His scruffy beard and mustache made him look a bit like her favorite rock musician. Kelly sighed happily. All the other girls were going to be so jealous of her handsome date.

"Hi!" Austin greeted her. His expression told Kelly he was as impressed with her appearance as she was with his. "All set to go?"

"Absolutely!" Kelly grinned widely.

"Great! I hope you don't mind if we run a quick errand first," Austin said. "My mother asked me to drop off some papers at her office."

"No problem," Kelly assured him. Since Dr. Vogel's office was in the same building as Lisa's parents', she knew it was right on their way to the beach.

While Austin held open the door of his car for her, Kelly slid inside. He had much nicer manners than Zack did. The only time Zack had ever played the gentleman was when they'd been dressed up for the junior prom.

But then, Austin was an older man. A college man. He obviously knew how to make a girl feel really special. With Austin she wasn't just one of the gang.

Austin drove quickly to his mother's office, zipping through two traffic lights just as they turned red. Kelly had her eyes closed tightly by the time he zoomed into the parking lot. When she felt it was safe to open them, she found herself facing a blue-and-white sign designating a handicapped parking place.

"Shouldn't you park somewhere else?" she asked. The doctors in the building had office hours on Saturdays, she knew, and many of the patients needed the handicapped spots.

"Don't worry," Austin insisted. "I'll just be a minute." He dashed off, leaving the motor running and his door open.

Well, Kelly decided, at least he'd left the keys. If someone needed this spot, she would move the car herself. It really wasn't very thoughtful of Austin to hog the spot, even if it was just for a minute.

The day was too pretty to waste worrying though. Kelly listened to the chirping of birds and the sounds of traffic on the street. She was going to enjoy herself today. She wouldn't even think about the conversation she'd overheard the night before.

"All set!" Austin declared, dropping back behind the wheel. "We're beach bound, babe."

Kelly giggled. Apparently even college guys got excited about a trip to the beach.

Austin had just backed his car up and headed back toward the street when a familiar car passed them.

"*Stop!*" Kelly yelled.

Austin slammed on his brakes. "What! Did I almost hit a dog or something?"

"No, no!" Kelly twisted to look back at the other car.

Austin sighed. "Whoa, that's a load off my mind. Well, let's go."

"That's my dad!" Kelly said, and frowned. The worry came flooding back. "What's he doing here?"

"Don't look at me," Austin recommended. "I've no idea. So, which is your favorite beach?"

Kelly glared at him. "But we can't go now," she insisted.

Austin looked puzzled. "Why not?"

"Because," she hissed urgently, "I have to find out what my dad is doing here. Maybe he's sick."

"Or maybe he's visiting that lawyer who just moved into the office next to Mom's," Austin mused.

Kelly's heart sank. "A *lawyer*?"

"Easy, kiddo," Austin said, and patted her knee in a consoling manner. "I know you don't want to admit your parents are breaking up, but it happens. Hey, mine have been divorced since I was ten. I didn't like it, either."

Kelly thought about how miserable her friend Jessie had been when her parents had broken up. Jessie had been hurt when her father had remarried, and not long ago she'd tried her best to ruin her mother's new romance. Kelly could see herself acting just as crazy, hoping that her parents would get back together again.

There was a difference between her situation and Jessie's or Austin's, though. They had been too young to do anything about their parents' divorces. But she wasn't. If they really *were* getting a divorce, that is.

Kelly pulled open the car door.

"Hey! Where are you going?" Austin yelled as she climbed out.

"I have to know what's going on," Kelly insisted. "I have to know if Dad really is going to see that lawyer."

Austin sighed. "You're nuts, you know."

"Maybe," Kelly said, and dashed off.

Chapter 10

▲　▼　▲　▼　▲

By noon Jessie couldn't stay still any longer. She had gone over all the materials on Desert Beauty that Sequoia and his sister had brought to the Green Teens meeting. She had read it so many times she could quote it all from memory. But was it all true? Could any company get away with hurting the environment with all the restrictions the government placed?

What she needed to do was talk to somebody about it all. But who?

Zack was the closest of her friends. He not only lived next door, but she had always felt like he was more of a brother than just a friend. Gathering up all the flyers, she dashed over to the Morrises'. And got the shock of her life.

"Zack is where?" she demanded, sure that she'd heard Mrs. Morris wrong.

"Las Vegas." Zack's mother looked up from the cookbook she had open on the kitchen counter. She grinned. "Awesome, isn't it."

"Yeah," Jessie agreed, stunned, and turned to wander back out the door. "Really awesome." It was just like Zack not to be available when she needed him.

Okay, Kelly! Jessie rushed back to her room, collapsed on the bed, and punched the Kapowskis' number up on her Princess phone.

Nicki Kapowski answered. "I think Kel went somewhere with that guy with the weird mustache. You want me to have her call you when she gets home?"

That wouldn't work. Jessie couldn't sit still waiting forever. Or at least what seemed like forever.

Slater. She argued with him a lot, but he was still a good friend.

"Sorry, Jessie," Mrs. Slater said when she answered the phone. "A. C. went to visit some new friends he met last night. Perhaps you know them? The Kilgore twins."

She was really striking out today, Jessie thought, her spirits sinking. Just when she needed them most, the whole gang seemed to have deserted her. She dialed another number. Somebody had to be home!

"Lisa!" Jessie gasped when she recognized a friendly voice. "I'm so glad I caught you. You wouldn't believe the troub—"

"Talk fast, girl," Lisa said, interrupting her. "I just heard there's a special unadvertised sale at the mall today, and I'm on my way out the door."

Jessie sighed. She knew it would be impossible to make an impression on Lisa as long as there was a shopping trip beckoning. "No, no. You go on."

Lisa must have sensed her disappointment. "Listen, if you need me, I'm there. Can you just wait a little bit? I'll meet you at the Max at three. Promise."

"Thanks, Lisa. I really need to talk to someone."

"I'll be all ears at three," Lisa vowed before flying off to the mall.

There were still hours to go, not only till she met Lisa but until the rendezvous with the Green Gremlins. How could she best fill the time? Trying to do homework was ridiculous. Jessie knew she couldn't keep her attention on any theme but the raid on Desert Beauty later that night.

A raid. It sounded so ... so ... so *destructive*! But that was exactly what Sequoia had termed the mission. And that's what had her worried.

She had agreed with him that time was short, that something had to be done. But did it have to be this? Sequoia had asked her if she just talked about saving the environment or if, when the time came, she was willing to do something about it. Feeling as if she would be failing as a dedicated member of Green Teens if she hesitated, Jessie had immediately declared she was up to whatever the Green Gremlins asked of her.

That had been last night. Now, without the mystery of the moonlight, the sound of the surf, and Sequoia's handsome face peering into hers, Jessie had doubts.

Get a grip, Spano. What was the first lesson she had ever learned from her mother? As a public defender, Mrs. Spano frequently had this same feeling that she didn't know all the facts. And she acted on it by . . . by . . . by what? Why was her mind being so contrary today? Had an evening on a romantic beach with Sequoia totally destroyed her thought processes?

But it had been so wonderful. Even if it had taken him all night to get around to kissing her. Then it had just been a fond peck on the cheek. Still, it had been fantastic.

Jessie sighed.

Research!

The word leaped into her mind. Of course! It was the perfect answer! She'd head for the library and find out all she could about laws to protect the desert. Then, when she met Lisa at the Max, she could talk out this pesky doubt she had and be fine by the time she saw Sequoia and the other Green Gremlins.

Relieved to be back in action, Jessie grabbed her purse and headed out the door.

▲   ▼   ▲

Kelly crept along the neatly trimmed hedge, careful to keep it between her and her father. She didn't know what she would do if he saw her. What could she say? She'd probably do something dumb like blurt out her fears, telling him that things couldn't be so bad that they couldn't work it out as a family. If she was that uncool, she'd just die of embarrassment.

Mr. Kapowski strode along the walkway, whistling as if he hadn't a care in the world.

How could he be so cheerful when her whole world was falling apart?

He took the steps to the main doors two at a time, eager to reach his appointment. He was so full of health that Kelly's last hope, that he had developed a serious disease, dissolved. Not that she wanted him to be sick, but sick and curable was better than having the family broken up by a divorce.

Kelly peered over the hedge, startling a gardener who had been pruning the bush. She and the gardener jumped in surprise. "Sorry," she mumbled, and edged closer to the wide glass doors of the lobby.

Her father stood peering at the building directory a moment, then entered the waiting elevator and punched a button.

The moment the doors slid closed, Kelly barrelled into the lobby.

Above the elevator door there was a row of numbers that lit up, indicating which floor the elevator stopped on. Holding her breath, Kelly watched as each brightened in succession until the numbers stopped changing and indicated someone getting off on the fourth floor. Her eyes swung to the directory. What offices were on that floor?

The board showed three: Dr. Vogel, family counseling; Drs. Turtle and Turtle, family practice; and R. Everhard, attorney-at-law.

Kelly was so involved that she didn't hear someone else enter the building and walk up to her. When a hand touched her arm, Kelly let out a scream.

"Hey, it's just me," Austin said. "Boy, are you jumpy."

"Oh, Austin," Kelly sighed in relief. "You were right! Look!" She pointed to the last listing for the fourth floor.

"Oh yeah. Mr. Everhard," Austin murmured. "He's new in private practice. Nice guy. I met him the other day. He handles personal injury cases as well as divorce, adoption, and estate planning. That's why he got an office in the same building with doctors and psychiatrists."

Kelly leaned back against the wall. "It's true, then. Oh, I was hoping it wasn't. But Dad wouldn't go to Lisa's parents since he has a special health plan where he works. And he wouldn't be going to see your mother alone, would he? Wouldn't a family counselor be working with all the family members?"

"Usually," Austin agreed. "Not always."

"That means he did go to see the lawyer. He was happy and cheerful and eager to go up there. He was whistling!" Kelly sank to the floor and put her forehead against her upraised knees. "I don't feel very well, Austin."

Austin hunkered down and patted her shoulder. "It's the shock after your rejection of the truth, that's all, Kelly. You'll be better in a little while." He gave her a smile of encouragement. "After all, you don't want your father to find you here when he comes back down, do you?"

Kelly jumped to her feet in a hurry, nearly knocking Austin over. "Gosh! No!" she cried, and rushed for the lobby door.

Austin ran to catch up with her as she dashed across the parking lot to his waiting car. "A day at the beach is just what you need, Kelly. You'll be relaxed and calm about this whole thing, and then—"

"Are you nuts?" Kelly demanded, yanking open the car door before Austin could reach it. "I can't go to the beach with you. I've got to find Jessie and do some serious talking!"

▲　▼　▲

"I can't believe it," Jessie said when Kelly tracked her down at the library. "Your parents are crazy about each other."

"I thought so, too," Kelly insisted, running her hands through her hair in distraction. She'd told

Austin to go to the beach without her. Who could concentrate on having fun at a time like this? "But I heard Mom and Dad talking about sending Billy away and having to make decisions about the rest of the family. What else could it be but a divorce?"

"Lots of things."

"Like what?"

"Ahh . . . well, there are tons of things it could be," Jessie insisted. "Maybe they were talking about vacation."

Kelly shook her head sadly. "We always do everything together."

"But maybe—"

Kelly straightened her shoulders. "If it is a divorce, I'll just have to be adult about this. I'll still love both my parents. I have to try to see their side of it."

"That's all very nice, but—"

Kelly forced a smile. "Let's not talk about it anymore. Instead tell me how your blind date went last night? What's Sequoia Forrest really like?"

"Are you sure you don't want to—"

"I'm sure," Kelly insisted. "So tell me everything. Did he kiss you?"

Jessie wrinkled her nose. "Sorta. But I'm sure he will later tonight."

"Great!"

"Well, maybe not so great," Jessie admitted. "I'm not sure anymore. I mean, I really believe in the same things Sequoia believes in, but I'm not so sure that what he wants to do is the right way to go about doing it. Do you understand?"

"Huh? Oh yeah."

Jessie grinned at her friend. "Come on. Let's go meet Lisa at the Max. Maybe she can give you some reason why your dad was hanging around her parents' office."

"Like coming down with a dreaded disease that only they can cure?" Kelly asked hopefully.

"Well, maybe we'll just buy you the largest hot fudge sundae, and you can drown your fears in calories," Jessie offered. "In fact, we'll get two spoons. I think I could use that kind of therapy myself."

▲　▼　▲

The triple fudge, six-scoop sundae was just a memory by the time Lisa got to the Max carrying an armload of packages.

"Uh-oh," she said, watching Kelly and Jessie both lick the last chocolate off their spoons. "Looks like you two have got some really major problemas."

"Tell us about it," Jessie declared. "Looks like you cleaned out a few stores."

Lisa scooted into the booth next to Kelly. "Well, I needed something to take my mind off guys. Last night I went to the dance with Brett Butler, and he was a total jerk."

"Men," Jessie groaned. "Sometimes I think life would be much easier without them."

"Easier maybe," Kelly said. "But not much fun."

"Is that ever a mouthful," Lisa agreed, and brightened up. "So, tell me how your blind dates went."

Kelly's smile drooped. "Mine told me my parents are getting a divorce."

"Mine wants me to break the law," Jessie said.

"What?" Lisa and Kelly demanded in unison.

"You didn't tell me that before," Kelly accused.

Jessie looked down at the table and drew circles on the surface. "Sequoia doesn't see it as breaking the law, but that's what it amounts to." She leaned closer to her friends. "Listen, you have got to swear you won't tell anyone about this."

"I swear," Kelly promised.

"Me, too," Lisa added. "On my charge card, so you know this is as good as forgotten, girlfriend."

"I swear, too," Screech announced, popping up from the booth behind Jessie.

The girls all stifled screams.

"Don't do that," Lisa growled.

"What are you doing here?" Jessie demanded. "Shouldn't you be off collecting bugs or something?"

Screech gave her one of his wide, elastic grins. "Nice of you to think about my collection, Jessie, but I'll soon have a large family of ladybugs. We're expecting," he admitted proudly.

"You mean you're going to have baby ladybugs?"

"Well," Screech said shyly, "I think there was one

daddy bug, too." He leaned farther over the back of the booth. "So, what's the big secret?"

Jessie looked at each of her friends in turn. "Sequoia and his sister Evergreen are heads of an undercover group called the Green Gremlins."

"Gosh!" Screech breathed.

"Golly!" Lisa gasped. "How did you find out?"

"He asked me to join them," Jessie said. Quickly she told them about Sequoia and his sister and what he had told her the night before. "They want me to be one of the lookouts on their mission tonight. The plan is to break into Desert Beauty's offices and wipe out their computer files."

"But that's destruction of private property, Jessie," Kelly said. "I don't think it's right that this company is selling off all the desert plants, but what the Green Gremlins are planning is really wrong. If you got caught, you could go to jail."

Jessie took a deep breath. "I know. Having a mom who is a public defender isn't going to help me, either. In fact, if something does go wrong, I could ruin her career."

"Ewww," Lisa said. "That's right. Talk about really being in hot water with a parent! It gives me goosebumps just thinking about it."

"I agree," Screech declared. "And I find it very hard to believe that someone named Christmas Tree could be mixed up in something of this magnitude."

Lisa frowned at him. "That's Evergreen, dork.

And anyone who has so little fashion sense as to dye her hair green is capable of doing anything this dastardly."

"Lisa's right," Kelly said.

"About the green hair?" Screech asked.

"About everything," Kelly answered. "You don't know these people well enough to get involved in this, Jessie."

"But Desert Beauty has to be stopped," Jessie insisted. "By the time the Green Teens march is organized, they could have sold off all the plants. We'd be too late to stop them."

Lisa tapped a finger against her cheek in thought. "You know," she mused, "when our neighbors had a pool put in last year, they landscaped with desert plants. If I remember right, there were certain rules or laws or something they had to follow in doing so."

Jessie nodded. "That's right. I found out about them when I was at the library. But it takes time and lots of paperwork to stop anyone that way. Sequoia insists that the Gremlins cut through all the red tape."

"What you need is a different plan, that's all," Kelly said. "Let's get hold of Zack and—"

"No can do," Jessie announced. "Morris went to Vegas with that Valley bimbo."

"You mean Brandi," Screech said. "She's really a very nice girl."

"Shut up, or I'll have to hurt you," Lisa told him.

Screech gave her a happy smile. "Whatever you say, my darling."

"Then Slater can help," Kelly suggested.

"Think again," Jessie said as the front door of the Max swung open and Slater waltzed in with a giggling redhead on each arm.

Lisa frowned in disgust. "Men are pigs," she declared.

"Boy, are they," Kelly agreed.

"I'll say," Jessie said.

"Disgusting," Screech announced. "I couldn't agree with you more."

"Screech, you're one of them," Lisa reminded him. "Or at least I think you are."

"Golly! You're right, my darling! I'm scum."

"Yes," Lisa said. "You are." She leaned forward. "All right, ladies, it's up to us."

Chapter 11

▲ ▼ ▲ ▼ ▲

Las Vegas was more than Zack had ever dreamed it could be. The desert stretched out to cover a wide valley hedged in by mountains in all directions. The sky was a clearer blue than that along the coast of California, and the temperature was at least twenty degrees warmer than in Palisades.

Nature wasn't the only thing that differed greatly. Massive parking lots, scads of hotels that rose taller than thirty floors, and bumper-to-bumper traffic greeted their arrival. Large signs proudly announced a variety of big-name stars appearing in the showrooms and different types of gambling.

"This place really is one big amusement park for adults," Zack said, awed by all that he saw.

"Yeah. The only real bummer about the place," Brandi agreed. "But it's getting better. When I was little, the only place kids could go was the circus midway. We could watch the circus acts that were performed over the casino floor but couldn't do much else. Now, in the summer, Wet and Wild, the waterpark next to the Sahara Hotel, is pretty boss, and a bungee jumping place isn't far from there. Daddy used to have a boat, so we spent a lot of time at Lake Mead, and in the winter, we'd go to Mount Charleston or snow skiing on the slopes in Lee Canyon."

Zack began to see why Brandi thought there wasn't much to do in Palisades.

"Of course," Brandi said, "if you're into the great outdoors, there's horseback riding at Bonny Springs and hiking in Red Rock Canyon or the Valley of Fire."

There really was more to Las Vegas than just the bright lights, Zack realized.

"You aren't into sports that much, are you?" Brandi asked.

Zack shrugged, trying to maintain a cool exterior although it felt like his insides were jumping up and down in excitement. "I'm on Bayside's track team and I surf a bit," he said modestly.

"I just asked because there's about a zillion golf courses, some league teams, and the sporting events at the university to see if you want. Not that there's a lot of time to do much this weekend, but I'm sure Daddy could arrange tickets to something if you're interested," Brandi offered.

Zack sighed in ecstasy. Weekends usually went by far too fast, but this one was really going to be over at warp speed.

"I'm easy," he said, his head filled with visions of hiking, a sports event, and some major time at the theme park they'd passed. "Whatever you want to do is fine with me."

"Super," Brandi breathed happily, "because all I really want to do is hang out at the pool."

Zack's jaw dropped open in disbelief. She had to be kidding.

"Well, maybe we can hit a few places later tonight, too," Brandi added, although she didn't sound very enthusiastic about showing him around.

Following her directions, Zack soon drove the Ferrari through the high gates of an exclusive condominium complex. The lush landscaping reminded him more of Palisades than of a place in the middle of the desert. A long stretch of dark green lawn rolled away toward reflecting pools and fountains. Tall palm trees, swaying eucalyptus trees, and flowering bushes were everywhere, lining driveways and sheltering broad patios.

The Jarretts' condo was near the large clubhouse and its Olympic-size pool. Mr. Jarrett was waiting for them at a table on the patio under a large umbrella.

He got to his feet as soon as he spotted the bright red sports car.

"Brandi! Zack! Did you have a good trip?"

"The best, Daddy," Brandi declared, giving him a quick hug.

"How was the drive, son?" Mr. Jarrett asked, shaking Zack's hand. "Not too long, I hope."

"Not in a Ferrari, sir," Zack assured him.

Mr. Jarrett laughed. "I didn't think you'd mind that part of the trip. Let's hope we can keep you as entertained for the rest of your stay. I've made reservations for dinner that include a jousting tournament at the Excalibur," he told them. The Excalibur Hotel was built to resemble a fairy-tale castle. Zack had caught a glimpse of it as they had exited the interstate earlier.

"After that, you tell me what you'd like to see," Brandi's father said. "But, until it's time to leave, perhaps you'd both like to cool off in the pool."

"Now, that sounds great," Zack agreed, wiping sweat from his forehead. He enjoyed warm weather as much as the next guy, but the desert temperature was over a hundred degrees.

"After dinner I have some people to see, so I'll let you show Zack around, Brandi," Mr. Jarrett said.

Brandi frowned. "Uh-oh. Doesn't sound like things went well at your meeting this afternoon."

"Just a little problem," Mr. Jarrett assured her. "Nothing for you to worry about, pumpkin. Now why don't you go enjoy your swim?"

To Zack those were the sweetest words he'd ever heard.

▲ ▼ ▲

"I don't like it," Brandi announced, sitting at poolside and dangling her long legs in the welcoming blue water. Zack had already swum two laps while she sunbathed.

"I know what you mean," Zack said, brushing his dripping hair back out of his face. "The water is as warm as a bath. I think I like the ocean better."

Brandi frowned at him. "This feels fine to me," she said, swishing her foot around in the pool. "Besides, that's not what I'm talking about. I mean Daddy. Something's wrong."

"Well, that's business," Zack declared. "Sometimes it's good, sometimes it's bad. I know because my dad recently started his own business and—"

Brandi wasn't paying attention to him. She looked off in the direction of the Jarretts' condo, her mind clearly on her father and his problems. "Daddy only comes to Vegas to escape business problems. Do you think it's easy faking his way through things at work? He's got ulcers from being at Inspirations, Inc."

"I suppose it would help to know something about computer animation," Zack agreed. "But your dad has probably learned a lot about it on the job."

"No, he hasn't. Why should he bother? I mean,

it's a scam, isn't it? But he's worried about something entirely different this time. I can tell," Brandi said.

Zack treaded water. "So what's the problem? With our brains, I'm sure the two of us can help him out."

"Maybe," Brandi agreed absently. "I think Daddy's in financial trouble. He's probably been gambling again and is worried that if Inspirations hears about it, he'll lose his job."

"Uh-oh. Good-bye vice presidency," Zack murmured.

"Not that I care about that," Brandi said. "Daddy got this stupid idea that I needed a settled, normal life, and that's why we moved to Palisades. We've been there for three years, but as far as I'm concerned, we were better off before."

Life before Palisades. The idea alone was spooky, Zack thought.

"Wouldn't you feel bad if you had to leave Valley High and your friends?" he asked.

"No, why should I?" Brandi answered. How would he feel if his father suddenly announced that they were leaving Palisades? Zack wondered. What would it be like to know he'd never have to avoid the Bayside hall monitors ever again? Would never have to report to Mr. Belding's office or to detention ever again? Never see Kelly or Jessie or Lisa or Screech or Slater ever again?

Terrible, that's how. Major mega-terrible.

"What's Valley got to offer you, right?" Zack said, trying to see Brandi's side of it all. She hadn't grown up in Palisades and known the same friends all her life like he had. "I'll bet you'd rather go back to the school you were at before, huh? Be with your old friends."

"Boy, is that ever lame," Brandi said. "We moved around a lot, and I knew a lot of dippy kids but no one I'd call a lifelong friend. It was no loss leaving any of them, Zack. Trust me. Being on the road is too much of a blast to be longing for all those places we stopped at along the way."

Slater's dad was in the armed forces and had moved their family around a lot. But Slater always said that kind of life was the pits. It didn't sound to Zack like Brandi would agree.

She stared off across the pool, but Zack didn't think Brandi was actually seeing any of the other people sunbathing around it. She chewed on her bottom lip thoughtfully and swung her feet back and forth in the water, nearly kicking him on the chin. Zack reached for safety at the side of the pool but stayed in the water where it was a slight bit cooler.

"You know," Brandi mused. "I'll bet Daddy's hit a snag over the sale of this place."

"He's selling the condo?" Zack echoed in surprise. There wasn't a realtor's sign out front.

"Has to, to pay off his gambling debts," Brandi said as if doing so were a common occurrence.

"Could be he couldn't get the price he needed."

"Well, that's out of our league," Zack said. Actually, he felt a little relieved that there wasn't much he could do to help Brandi and her father. Scamming was great, but it sounded as if the Jarretts did more than just that. Constantly being on the move made their life seem more like they were running away before they got caught doing something illegal.

Or at least like they had done something illegal in the past. Mr. Jarrett was determined to make a better life for Brandi and had done what seemed to be the most logical thing to him. While it was impressive that he'd scammed his way into a top position with Inspirations, Inc., it didn't sound like Brandon Jarrett was actually enjoying his newfound success.

"You know," Brandi said, her voice pitched to a thoughtful tone.

Zack's friends could have warned him about that sound. They'd heard him use it often enough. It meant a scam was hatching.

"I think we can help Daddy," Brandi declared. "All we have to do is . . ."

His heart sinking, Zack listened as she spelled out her plan. It had possibilities, but what happened if they got caught?

Zack fazed out, his imagination painting a picture of how he'd look in striped prison clothes. How it would feel to live behind bars.

Zack clutched at the bars with both hands. "Hhheeellllpppp!" he whispered.

"Zack?"

Zack popped out of his dream and back to reality. "Oh, Brandi. Ah, yeah, sure. Of course we've got to help your dad. You can count on me," he said, and swallowed loudly. "After all, maybe I'll be very good at making license plates," he mumbled under his breath.

"What did you say?" Brandi asked.

"Ah, that I hope they have really big plates at dinner. Boy, am I hungry."

And, boy, am I in big trouble. Zack let go of the side of the pool and sank under the water. Maybe if he was lucky, he'd just drown now.

Chapter 12

▲ ▼ ▲ ▼ ▲

The moon hung high in the California night sky, spilling silver light over the desert floor. Deep shadows made it impossible to identify most of the plants that sheltered close to the ground. Only the Joshua trees stood out clearly, looking like statues of weird alien cheerleaders carrying pom-poms. Although frozen at the moment, they looked like they might jump to life and give a mighty cheer.

What would it be? Jessie wondered, as she inched along behind Sequoia through the underbrush. *Give 'em heck, give 'em flack! Make Desert Beauty never come back! Goooo Gremlins!* Or would it be *Don't be down, don't give ground! Stop Desert Beauty by making a sound! Goooo Spano!*

If the Joshua trees weren't rooting for her, Jessie knew that at least the gang was.

Unless Screech had fallen into a bed of snoozing cactus, that is. Rescuing him from a nest of desert stickers would distract Lisa and Kelly from their own mission.

Since she hadn't heard any unearthly screams of pain filling the night, Jessie figured that her secret-agent friends were in place and waiting.

They'd better be. If not, she was going to look really foolish really soon.

In front of her, Sequoia stopped and hunkered down behind a thick clump of tangled tumbleweed. The desert camouflage clothing he wore made him blend into the landscape well. Only the bark color of his hair stood out. His broad muscular shoulders were a lot more substantial than anything growing in the desert, too.

Without looking back at the rest of his cohorts, Sequoia motioned them to halt. Jessie almost expect-ed some of the Green Gremlins to walk into each other in the dark. There were a couple of them who looked as clumsy and uncoordinated as the members of the Bayside chess club. When he introduced them to her, Sequoia had termed them techno-specialists, but they looked like pencil-toting computer nerds to Jessie. They were under Evergreen's command and were the geniuses who were to crash the Desert Beauty computer system.

Unless Jessie stopped them.

And if she failed? What would Sequoia,

Evergreen, and the other Gremlins do to her? She
was the newest member, an untried member, and
she'd already finked on them.

Well, not exactly, but close enough.

Jessie looked at Sequoia's handsome profile and
sighed quietly to herself. He was just the kind of guy
she would like to be with. They had so much in common. But he might see her work that night as rather
traitorous.

But it wasn't. It was law-abiding. And if the
gang's plan worked, they'd be heroes.

If not, their names would be mud.

"There it is," Sequoia said, his voice barely audi-
ble. He parted the tumbleweed bushes so that those
behind him could see their objective.

The long, low building of adobe brick didn't look
very impressive or sinister. In fact, it looked like
somebody's home. Warm lamplight lit the two front
windows. A yellow porch light glowed near the door.
The front area had been landscaped with various low-
growing cactus plants, some in Mexican-style clay
pots, and a walkway constructed of wide red tiles. To
the back of the building another porch light high-
lighted row upon row of desert plants, their roots
wrapped in bundles of soil and burlap.

There was no high electric fence. No guard dogs.
No patrolling security men.

Apparently Desert Beauty wasn't too worried
about anyone stealing their plants. Maybe that was

because they were five miles from the closest neighbor and located on a dirt road far from the main highway.

"All right," Sequoia said, turning to face his troops. "We don't want any mistakes. Right?"

"Right," Jessie echoed. Certainly no big mistakes that would ruin her life. Which this was sure to do if something went wrong.

Evergreen frowned and pushed a stray lock of green hair back under the dark baseball cap she wore. "You're wasting time, Sequoia," she insisted.

Waste it, Jessie urged silently. *Waste lots of time.* She glanced at her watch. The hands didn't seem to be moving. What if her watch had stopped? What if she messed up on the timing and ruined everything?

"Timing is important," Sequoia told his sister.

You said it, bub, Jessie thought.

"Algernon, once Evergreen disconnects the electronic security system, I'll pick the lock on the door. You've got the layout of the place memorized?"

Algernon, who was even skinnier than Screech, pushed his glasses up and tapped a finger against his forehead. "Blueprints are all laid out up here, chief," he said.

"Right," Sequoia said. "Once the door is open, you proceed to the main office and override Desert Beauty's passwords and other security features."

Algernon saluted with his left hand and knocked his glasses off. It took everyone three minutes to find them for him in the dark. It would have taken longer if after Jessie found the glasses and tossed them over her shoulder, they hadn't landed on the ground right under Evergreen's searching fingers.

Once Algernon had regained his sight, Sequoia turned to the chubby boy who crouched near Evergreen. "You follow Algernon, Percy," Sequoia ordered. "Erase any messages on the phone system and then disconnect the phone lines. They have at least four of them, so make sure you get them all."

Percy nodded slowly.

"By then Algernon will have the files pulled up. Working on different terminals, you will download everything onto our diskettes so we have records of everyone Desert Beauty has done business with."

Jessie's mouth nearly fell open in shock. She hadn't realized the Green Gremlins were planning on stealing information as well as destroying it. What were they planning to do with it? She really needed to stop them!

"There has been one slight change in our original plans," Sequoia announced. "I learned that Desert Beauty also keeps hard-copy files. So, I want Evergreen and Jessie to help me empty the file cabinets and pile all the records in the courtyard where we can burn them," Sequoia said.

"Burn them? Me?" Jessie croaked. "But I thought I was supposed to be just a lookout!"

"Think of this as the perfect chance to prove

yourself to the rest of us," Evergreen insisted, and gave Jessie a look that was filled with suspicion. "Some of us aren't as trusting about your devotion to the cause as my brother is."

Think fast, Spano, Jessie urged herself.

She glared at the green-haired Gremlin commander. "Some of us are smart enough to know that having a lookout is a very important part of any mission. I think it is dangerous *not* to have one, that's all," Jessie explained, faking her anger over Evergreen's suspicions.

"Jessie's right," Sequoia said.

Whew! Jessie sighed in relief.

"But we don't have the Gremlin power to spare, so we'll all have to keep on the alert," he added.

Drat. Foiled again.

Jessie tried to grab a glance at her watch without the others noticing, but it was too dark to see if the time to confess what she'd done had arrived yet or not.

Evergreen noticed her action, though. "What's the matter, Jessie? Got a late date?" she sneered. "Or did you perhaps sell us out?"

Uh-oh. Maybe it was best to come clean.

"Listen," Jessie said. "I don't like this operation. It isn't right what you're planning to do."

Sequoia straightened, his head turned toward the road. He made a motion for quiet, but Jessie ignored it.

"I know Desert Beauty has got to be stopped," Jessie insisted. "There are other ways, though. Legal ways."

"Shh," Sequoia hissed. "Listen."

At first Jessie could hear nothing but the soft noises of the desert night. A gentle breeze rustled the feathery-branched bushes. A small animal scampered away nearby. Then she heard it. The sound of car engines.

"I knew it," Evergreen hissed. "She did fink on us." She melted away into the shadows, followed silently by the two nerds.

Jessie turned quickly to Sequoia and put her hand on his arm, stopping him before he could disappear, too. "I didn't give you away," she said softly. "Please believe me, Sequoia. But I couldn't go through with this plan. You can't right one wrong by doing another one. Stopping Desert Beauty by destroying their files would have been only a temporary solution."

"And you have a better idea, is that it?" Sequoia demanded angrily. He pulled away from Jessie's restraining hand.

"Yes!" Jessie cried. "I used the most efficient system for getting things done in this country. I networked!"

Sequoia snorted in disgust. "Networked? You mean you called somebody to get a favor? That's a joke."

"No, it isn't," Screech insisted, jumping from his hiding place. He pointed a long, dark piece of plastic at the hulking leader of the Green Gremlins. "Freeze, mister. Perhaps I should warn you. This water bazooka is loaded with 100% mineral water. I went heavy on the iron content so it would pack a wallop."

Lisa stepped from behind another bush, holding another heavy-duty squirt gun. "And mine's filled with the cheapest perfume I could find. One squirt of this stuff and not even a lovesick skunk will come near you, honey."

Sequoia spun around only to be confronted with Kelly. In her hand she balanced a whipped-cream pie. "Take one more step and make my day," she threatened.

Sequoia turned back to Jessie, his hands clenched in angry fists at his sides. "What now, Jessie? Is that the cops coming? Is that who you networked with?"

"No! Of course it isn't!" Jessie cried. "I networked with the network. The television network."

Sequoia looked suspicious but also a little puzzled.

"Listen to me, Sequoia," Jessie continued more calmly. "The way to get fast action on anything is to call in a tip to 'You Witness Crime,' the news show. Those are their cameras and reporters arriving."

"And you think I believe you?" Sequoia snapped.

"I trusted you, Jessie, and you betrayed that trust."

"No, I didn't," Jessie said. "I just saw a better way to achieve what we wanted. After you tell the cameras the truth about Desert Beauty's business, there is no way they will be able to sell off any more plants."

"*Me?* What do you mean, me?" he asked.

"Yeah," Lisa said. She shouldered her megapowered squirt gun. "Why should he do it? You're the one who saved the day, Jessie."

"You tell her, babe," Screech advised. "After all, if Jessie's mother hadn't gone to high school with the director of 'You Witness Crime,' we never would have gotten the camera crew out here in the middle of the night."

Jessie stared up into Sequoia's moss green eyes. "All I did was network," she said. "But I'm not the one who knows all the details about Desert Beauty. You are, Sequoia. You need to be the one representing our cause. Not as a Green Gremlin but as a Green Teen."

Sequoia hesitated.

"This way cuts through red tape, too," Jessie reminded him. "And once you talk to them, you'll have your own networking source."

Car doors slammed, and a bright search light lit the whole area. Jessie could hear the noise of equipment being unloaded. "Hello?" a man's voice called. "Is anybody there?"

"Are you with me?" Jessie held out her hand to Sequoia.

The silence stretched between them for what seemed like an eternity. At last, his fingers closed over hers. "Yeah," he said. "I guess I am."

"We'll be right there!" Jessie called out to the waiting camera crew.

As she and Sequoia walked out to the road hand in hand, Lisa sighed loudly. "Well, I'm glad that's over."

"Me, too," Screech agreed. "I never realized mineral water was so heavy before." The long plastic end of his squirt gun tipped to point at the desert floor.

"My arm is getting tired, too," Kelly admitted. "What should I do with this pie? I can't just leave it here. That's littering."

"So true," Lisa said, then jumped back to avoid getting hit with Screech's squirt gun as he turned to peer out at the TV crew. "Look out!" she yelled as she stumbled against Kelly.

"What?" Screech asked, glancing back over his shoulder at the girls.

Losing her balance, Kelly fell forward. But the cream pie in her hand sailed upward.

Right into Screech's face.

"Well," Lisa said as she helped Kelly to her feet. "It looks like we don't have to worry about what to do with the pie after all."

"Guess not," Screech agreed happily. He scraped some of the whipped cream off his face with a finger and tasted it. "Hmm. Next time, though," he suggested, "let's get chocolate."

Chapter 13

▲ ▼ ▲ ▼ ▲

Overnight a herd of butterflies had taken up residence in Zack's stomach. Now they wanted out! Or so it felt to Zack.

He wasn't sure if the weird feeling was a result of his bungee jumping and all the wild rides he'd gone on at the MGM theme park the night before, or if it was a result of being roped into playing the major part in Brandi's scheme to help her father.

Whatever the answer, the nervous fluttering in his middle nearly ruined Zack's appreciation of the monster-size breakfast buffet Brandi and her father took him to Sunday morning. After filling his plate three times, Zack entirely lost his appetite.

But he had to agree with Brandi that Mr. Jarrett was definitely worried about something. Brandi's dad joked and laughed, but when he thought Zack and his daughter weren't watching him, his smile faded to a sad, anxious look. He didn't seem very happy.

In fact, Zack decided, Mr. Jarrett looked kind of scared.

Was that what it was like to be an adult scammeister?

It was spooky enough being a teenage scammeister! Especially when he got caught.

That wasn't something Zack cared to think about right now. Especially if he was going to successfully pull off his part in Brandi's scheme.

If he wasn't relaxed, Brandi sure was. She chattered away as Zack drove the Ferrari through a quiet residential neighborhood. It reminded him of those in Palisades. Kids played in the yards and rode their bikes along the sidewalks. They all stopped to stare after the Ferrari as it drove by.

Or maybe they were staring at him. Zack was sure none of his friends would recognize him. His jeans looked like they'd been through a shredder, his black shirt was missing all its buttons and hung open, fingerless leather gloves covered his hands, and his usually carefully styled blond hair looked like it had been arranged with the help of an eggbeater. With a fake tattoo on his cheek and another one on his forearm, probably even Bayside tough guy Denny Vane would think twice about crossing this Zack Morris.

Zack sure wouldn't want to run into himself in a dark alley.

"This is it," Brandi said, pointing to a neat little house on the corner. Rosebushes lined the walkway. A big yellow cat was curled up in the front window. It watched them approach, then yawned, and went back to its nap.

The butterflies went nuts again. Zack took a deep breath trying to calm them. He could do this. It was easy. All he had to do was con somebody's grandmother.

Not good, Morris. But he'd promised to help Brandi help her dad. There was no way out. "Ready when you are, babe," Zack said in a gruff voice.

"It will be a snap," Brandi assured him. "You look like totally bad."

"Thanks. I think," Zack said.

Brandi bounced out of the car. Zack climbed out more slowly, his steps dragging. Brandi linked arms with him and forced him to move faster up the walk. She leaned on the bell.

"Mrs. Rushforth?" she asked when an elderly woman answered the door. "I'm Brandi Jarrett. I talked to you on the phone last night."

"Oh yes. About your father's condominium, wasn't it, dear?" Mrs. Rushforth said. "Won't you come in?"

"Thanks. I hope you don't mind that I brought along a friend. This is Zachariah Hellfire. Perhaps you've heard of him? He's the drummer for the heavy metal rock group Weirder Beasts."

"Yo," Zack said.

"Ah, yo to you, too, young man," Mrs. Rushforth greeted him, trying not to stare at the drawing of a snake on his face. "I'm afraid I'm not familiar with your music."

"'No Sweat,'" Zack grunted.

"Yes, I do try to keep it nice and cool in the house," Mrs. Rushforth said.

"No, like that was the name of our big hit," Zack drawled.

"Oh." Mrs. Rushforth looked at him blankly. "I'm afraid I'm not familiar with that particular tune."

"No sweat," Zack said.

"Yes, dear. You already told me the title."

"No, I mean, that's all right," Zack explained.

"Oh," Mrs. Rushforth said a bit uncertainly, and turned to Brandi. "Please take a seat. Both of you. Would you like some iced tea?"

Brandi shook her head and pulled Zack down to sit with her on the sofa. "Nothing, thank you. We'll just keep you a minute, Mrs. Rushforth."

"It's no trouble, dear," the elderly woman assured her as she perched on the edge of a chair. "Now, what was it you wanted to see me about, Miss Jarrett?"

"You've been considering buying my father's condo, haven't you, Mrs. Rushforth?" Brandi asked.

A soft smile warmed Mrs. Rushforth's face. "My

daughter and her husband have urged me to. I believe you know them. They own the condo next to yours."

Brandi nodded.

"They'd like me to live closer to them," Mrs. Rushforth continued. "And, the truth is, I would enjoy not having to do yard work anymore. But the price your father is asking is a bit more than I'd like to spend."

"So you aren't interested anymore?" Brandi asked.

"I don't believe so," the elderly woman answered.

Brandi gave her a big smile. "Oh, I'm so glad you said that," she declared, and tossed Zack an adoring look. "You see, Mr. Hellfire is interested in buying it, too, and we wanted to make absolutely sure that you didn't mind. Daddy said that he promised you the first chance on the condo. But since you don't want it, Zachariah can take it."

She turned to face Zack, nearly bouncing with excitement. "Isn't this wonderful? Now you don't have to find another place for the band to practice. You can move in and rehearse any time you want."

"All right!" Zack agreed. "My skins can be set up in no time."

Mrs. Rushforth's hands fluttered in her lap. "Skins? What did you say you play, Mr. Hellfire?"

"Drums," Zack said. "The biggest, meanest, loudest set you ever saw. It's really bad."

"You play badly?"

"No, I play a lot to make sure that I don't," Zack assured her. "Last place I lived had this really boss chandelier thing, you know. Vibrations from my skins sent the thing crashing. It was awesome."

"Vibrations?" Mrs. Rushforth repeated faintly.

Brandi leaned forward. "Oh, you're thinking about the value of your daughter's condo, aren't you," she soothed. "Daddy was a little worried about that, too, but, I mean, like how could anything bad happen? Scads of people will want to live next door to the drummer for Weirder Beasts."

"They will?" Mrs. Rushforth didn't sound as convinced of this.

"Absolutely."

Zack gave the elderly woman a smile. "If your daughter and her family want to like hang out with me and the band, it would be cool. We've always got a party going on, especially when we do late-night jams. Once we get all the amplifiers set up, the sound is like sonic."

"Sonic?"

"You can come, too," Zack invited. "We could like play some oldies for you. Who's your favorite group? The Rocket Silos? Bomb Baskets?"

Mrs. Rushforth sank back in her chair. "I don't suppose you've ever heard of Percy Mincestep and the Toe-Tapping Music Makers?"

"Hmm," Zack mused. "Percy Mincestep and the Toe-Tapping Music Makers. Did they ever have an album go platinum?"

"I don't think so," Mrs. Rushforth said.

"Well, this is totally awesome, isn't it?" Brandi demanded, getting to her feet. "Come on, Zachariah. Let's get back to the condo so you can sign the deal with Daddy. The sooner you can move in the better, right?"

"Yo," Zack answered.

"Thank you for seeing us, Mrs. Rushforth," Brandi gushed as she pulled Zack with her to the door.

"Yeah," Zack added. "And don't forget to come to one of my parties. There's one every night, all night, so it doesn't matter when you stop by."

"Oh dear," Mrs. Rushforth murmured. "It was most . . . ah . . . interesting meeting you, Mr. Hellfire," she called as she waved good-bye to them.

Brandi slid into the Ferrari and waved back while Zack climbed behind the wheel. A happy grin curved her lips. "You were fantastic," she announced. "I'll bet she's on the phone to her daughter right this minute."

"Yeah," Zack said. He started the engine, but this time it didn't feel as great to be driving the expensive sports car.

"Aw, what's the matter, Zacky?" Brandi purred. "Didn't you get a rush out of scamming her?"

"She's a nice lady," he said.

"So? Daddy needs to close this deal. Now it will close with a real nice snap. There is no way that lady will let someone like Zachariah Hellfire move in next door to her daughter's family."

"Yeah," Zack agreed with a sigh. "You got what you wanted."

"Oh, lighten up, will you, Morris?" Brandi said. "With that long face, you'd think we did something wrong or something."

"Yeah," Zack mumbled. He didn't think they had. He *knew* they had. And he didn't like knowing that.

▲ ▼ ▲

Zack was back to normal an hour later. Brandi had gone off for another session of sunbathing by the pool. Mr. Jarrett was packing his things. With only an hour left before the flight back to Palisades, Zack took the one chance he had and slipped next door to the condo where Mrs. Rushforth's daughter lived and rang the bell.

A slender woman answered the door. She reminded Zack a lot of his mother.

"Hi," Zack said, then glanced back toward the pool area to make sure Brandi couldn't see him. "I don't have much time. I've got to ask you a question, but I can't be seen doing it."

The woman holding the door looked suspicious.

"It's about Mrs. Rushforth," Zack confessed quickly.

"Mother? Is something wrong?"

Feeling like he would be found out any minute, Zack hastened to reassure her. "Oh no. At least not yet. Did she call you about buying Mr. Jarrett's condo?"

Mrs. Rushforth's daughter didn't say a word.

It was much easier to right a wrong when you were a comic book hero, Zack decided. He didn't think he'd look any more sincere wearing a cape and tights, though. Probably less so. And time was running out. He had to fix this wrong right now.

"Listen. There is no rock music drummer moving in next door. You don't have to worry about that. So, if Mrs. Rushforth doesn't want the Jarretts' condo, don't worry. I'm pretty sure that Mr. Jarrett won't sell it to anybody you don't like."

"Who are you?" Mrs. Rushforth's daughter demanded.

"Just a friend of your mother's," Zack said quickly.

"Really." She didn't sound as if she believed that one.

Brandi would be headed back to the condo any minute. If she caught him confessing, his reputation as a master scammer was over.

"I just don't want a nice lady like her to get cheated by paying too much for the condo, that's all," Zack declared.

"Oh, she wouldn't," Mrs. Rushforth's daughter assured him. "Mother was hoping to get Brandon to drop the price below market value. We all know he's desperate to sell."

It sounded to Zack like there had been more than just one scam going on.

"I told Mother she was gambling and would lose on this deal if she wasn't careful," Mrs. Rushforth's daughter said. "I was pleased when she called and told me she'd give Brandon the price he was asking. It was a fair one." She smiled suddenly. "Probably only because he knows Mother is a schemer just like he is. Is it because you know him that you were worried about my mother?"

"Ah, not exactly," Zack said, relieved that things were working out as they should despite his and Brandi's interference.

"Mother will enjoy knowing she had a young champion concerned about her. What's your name?"

Zack backed away from the door. "Ah, I'm nobody, really," he insisted. "Just . . . just . . . er . . . tell her Zack said hi."

"She'll know who you are by that?"

Boy, will she!

Chapter 14

▲ ▼ ▲ ▼ ▲

Kelly lay in bed with the pillow over her head on Sunday. It was D day—the day she was going to ask her parents about the D-I-V-O-R-C-E. All she had to do was work up her courage and plan the best course of action.

What could she say to them? "Hey, what's this I hear about a divorce?" No. Too perky. "Stay together, please! If not for yourselves, then for us kids!" Too pathetic and melodramatic.

She had to think of something, and fast. It was driving her nuts thinking about it. Part of her insisted her family couldn't be breaking up, but there was another part of her that was afraid that Austin was right. After all, why else would her mom and dad have talked about splitting their children up? And why would her dad go see a lawyer? They must be getting a divorce.

Well, there was only one way that she was ever going to know, and that was to ask them.

Kelly climbed out of bed, shoved her feet into her big, fluffy slippers, and headed for the kitchen.

For a change, there was no one in the room except her mom and dad. Both were sitting at the table sipping coffee and reading different sections of the newspaper.

Kelly plopped down in a chair between them. "Okay," she said. "Tell me why you are getting a divorce."

"A *divorce*?" Mr. Kapowski echoed.

"Who says we're getting a divorce?" Mrs. Kapowski demanded.

Kelly sighed. They were going to cover it up just so she wouldn't feel bad. Didn't they know she was nearly grown up? She could handle the bad news. She'd cry her eyes out and make them feel terrible, but she could handle hearing the worst.

"I heard you talking the other night," Kelly said. "About sending Billy away and how you had to arrange things for the rest of us, too."

Mrs. Kapowski smiled softly and reached over to pat Kelly's hand. "Don't worry, darling. We aren't—"

"Don't try to keep this from me, Mom. I followed you yesterday, Daddy. You went to see Mr. Everhard, that lawyer, didn't you?"

Mr. Kapowski glanced across the table at Kelly's

mother a moment before turning to his daughter. "Yes, I did, but, sweetheart—"

"Oh no!" Kelly cried. "Don't do it! I love you both so much." She jumped out of her chair and hugged each of her parents in turn. "I just know you could work things out if you just talked to someone. Maybe Dr. Vogel. That's Austin's mother. She's a family counselor. I could call her now."

"Darling—"

"It's no trouble," Kelly hastened to add. "Maybe she could even come over here. If she can't, I'll babysit whenever you need to go see her. I'll quit my job at Yogurt 4-U if necessary so I'm here when you need me."

"Kelly—"

"I mean it," Kelly said. "I'll call her now."

"Kelly," her mother said softly. "We aren't getting a divorce."

"You're not . . . ?"

"We're not," Kelly's father said. "I couldn't think of a worse thing to happen to me than to go through life without your mother to keep me in line."

Mrs. Kapowski grinned at him. "I do my best, dear," she said.

Relief flooded through Kelly, making her feel weak. She sank back into her chair. "Oh, I'm so glad."

"You jumped to conclusions without asking us for the truth." Mr. Kapowski shook his head slowly. "I thought we taught you better than that."

"We've never kept secrets from you or the rest of our children," Mrs. Kapowski reminded her.

Kelly hung her head. She did know better. Her family always had been truthful with one another. She should have just walked into the room the other night and asked what her parents were talking about. It would have saved her a lot of worry.

"So, what were you talking about?" Kelly asked, just a few days late.

"Our will," her dad answered.

A will! Kelly's spirits dropped. The ghost of an incurable, rare disease raised its head again.

Mr. Kapowski looked a bit sheepish. "You see, Kelly, your mother and I realized that we hadn't made any changes in it since your older brothers were babies. If something had happened to us, no provisions had been made for taking care of all of you."

"It wasn't an easy task deciding what we should do, darling," Mrs. Kapowski said. "Although you and your older brothers can take care of yourselves, we worried about the little ones."

"So you're going to break us up?" Kelly demanded. "You think that's what's best for everybody? How could you think that? We're a family. Families need to stay close to each other. We depend on each other, love each other."

"We know that," her mother assured her.

"And we knew that you'd feel that way, too, sweetheart," her father said.

Kelly stared at her parents. "But that didn't stop you from deciding to send us all to the ends of the earth, did it?" she declared. It was a sad day when a teenager had to be disappointed in her parents. "Is that what you went to tell Mr. Everhard yesterday? Remember, Daddy, I saw you, and you were so happy that you were whistling."

Mr. Kapowski smiled and leaned back in his chair. "Yes, I was," he agreed. "What I told him was that your mother and I wanted our children to stay together."

Kelly's eyes widened. "You did?"

"We simply named a guardian to watch over the younger ones. Someone we knew would do everything possible to care for them."

"You did?"

"It wasn't an easy choice," Mr. Kapowski said.

"But we know it was the right choice for our family," Mrs. Kapowski added.

"Of course it was," Kelly agreed, happy now that she knew everything was back to normal, that her parents still loved each other. All was right with her world. "So who'd you name? Aunt Shirley?"

Her parents shook their heads.

"Uncle Phil?"

"Nope."

Kelly frowned. "It wasn't Cousin Marvin from Topeka, was it?"

"We named you and Kirby," Mr. Kapowski said.

Mrs. Kapowski smiled. "After the fierce display of family pride you just gave us, why would you think we'd choose anyone else?"

Kelly threw herself into their arms. "Oh, thank you, thank you. I'll do my best. But, first, you have to promise that nothing will happen to you."

"Darling, you know we can't promise—" Mrs. Kapowski began.

A shout from the hall cut her off. "*Kelllyyy!* Telephone! It's some boy!"

Kelly's dad sighed loudly. "Isn't it always? If he wants to marry you, tell him I said the answer is no."

"Oh, Daddy," Kelly said with a giggle, then dashed for the phone.

▲ ▼ ▲

When the bell rang for lunch at school on Monday, the gang met in the cafeteria.

"Whew! I wasn't sure I could make it much longer without food," Zack declared, shoving a loaded tray onto the table.

"What's the matter?" Jessie cooed. "Tough weekend in Las Vegas?"

"Terrible one," Zack said.

"Yeah, I'll bet," Lisa sneered. "You were off having fun while we were out saving the world."

"*You*, Lisa? What did you do? Declare war on the color puce?" Zack asked with a laugh.

"At least we weren't hiding out from the football team," Jessie said. "I hear they made a tackle dummy that looks just like you, Zack."

Zack had heard the same rumor and had ducked English class to check it out. "It's just a surface resemblance," he insisted. "I think it looks more like Mr. Belding, myself."

"That's only because Butch ripped off the blond wig in practice this morning," Slater said, setting his lunch tray down and taking the seat nearest to Jessie. "I thought it was an excellent likeness of you."

Zack swallowed loudly.

"Hi!" Kelly greeted him, bouncing up to the table. "Isn't it a great day?"

"It's Monday," Slater pointed out.

"The absolute worst day of the week," Jessie reminded her.

Kelly slipped into the chair next to Lisa. "But my parents aren't getting a divorce, so it's a wonderful day!"

"Oh, Kelly! I'm so glad!" Lisa cried, and gave her friend a quick hug. "So you finally asked them."

Kelly beamed. "Yes, and Austin had it all wrong."

"Did you tell him?" Jessie demanded.

Kelly giggled. "Not only did I tell him, I slammed the phone down so hard when he called, I'll bet his ears are still ringing!"

Slater looked across the table at Zack. "Who's Austin?"

"Kelly's parents were getting a divorce?" Zack asked. "Boy, did I miss out on things!"

Screech rushed up to the table and passed out chocolate cigars. "I'm an uncle!" he announced with a wide grin.

Slater frowned at Zack. "How can he be an uncle when he's an only child?"

Zack shrugged.

"Oh, the ladybugs hatched!" Kelly cried excitedly.

"That's how," Zack told Slater.

"I should have guessed."

"And speaking of ladybugs," Jessie said, turning to Slater. "How are Courtney and Kimberly Kilgore?"

Slater groaned. "Don't ask. I thought it was bad enough with you always harping about your Green Teen projects, but I didn't realize what hell was until I heard it all in stereo. Remind me never to date twins again."

"You got it, honey," Lisa said. "What I want to hear is what happened with Sequoia and the television crew."

"Who or what is Sequoia?" Zack asked Slater.

"The correct word is *what*," Slater said. "And the answer is, a jerk."

"Really?" Screech said. "I don't think those reporters from 'You Witness Crime' thought so. They looked really interested in what he had to say."

Jessie nodded proudly. "They were. In fact, they've offered him a regular spot on their program to report on different environmental issues."

Lisa sighed dreamily. "Then everything ended

happily. Are you going to see Sequoia again?"

"No," Jessie said. "I don't think I can take another weekend like this one."

"Me neither," Kelly said. "From now on, I only date guys I know."

Zack brightened. "Hey, I like the sound of that!"

"What's the matter, Zack? Miss Valley High dump you?" Jessie asked.

Screech's eyes looked like they were ready to pop out of his head. "Wow! You mean Brandi was voted Miss Valley High, too? She deserves it. She's a really nice girl."

"Boy, are you wrong," Zack mumbled under his breath.

"Well, it's a new week," Slater said, stretching in his seat. "And that means we've got a new game. I hear that our opponent has one of the meanest backfields in the city and that running into them is like hitting a brick wall."

He leaned over the table and motioned to the rest of the gang to gather close. "Now if we could just find a way to keep a couple of these guys out of the game. . . ."

Everybody exchanged glances, then picked up their ammunition.

"Hey! Stop it, you guys!" Slater yelled when the first barrage of french fries hit him.

Nobody listened. They just threw more fries.